About the Author

Rose Staveley-Wadham is a young novelist who lives in London, although she retains strong links to the West Sussex countryside where she grew up.

She has been writing fiction since she was ten, and is extremely passionate about storytelling.

A graduate of Durham University, Rose completed a degree in English Literature, and is an avid reader. She also enjoys writing poetry.

When not writing, Rose enjoys walking in the West Sussex countryside, the countryside that inspires much of her work. She enjoys learning languages, researching her family tree, and socialising with friends.

The Red Dress

Rose Staveley-Wadham

The Red Dress

Olympia Publishers
London

www.olympiapublishers.com
OLYMPIA PAPERBACK EDITION

A CIP catalogue record for this title is
available from the British Library.

ISBN: 978-1-78830-053-7

This is a work of fiction.
Names, characters, places and incidents originate from the writer's
imagination. Any resemblance to actual persons, living or dead, is purely
coincidental.

First Published in 2018

Olympia Publishers
60 Cannon Street
London
EC4N 6NP
Printed in Great Britain

Dedication

For Oscar

Acknowledgments

With thanks to Margaret, my first reader and biggest support. Without your help, producing this work would have been impossible. Also, to my friends (who are too numerous to name here) and my family, who did not stop believing in me even when I had stopped believing in myself. Finally, Christopher and Marisa North, whose hospitality in beautiful Relleu, Spain, enabled me to write *The Red Dress*.

CHAPTER ONE

In spite of the conversation at the Radisson, Polly decided to marry him anyway. She was quite excited by the prospect of an understated ceremony at Islington town hall, an event that Charles Carraway had already organised for her. Polly's marriage would then take place precisely a week after her graduation, and by that time it would be July.

She laughed a little at the thought of it. There were all her friends, if friends they could be called, scrambling around for graduate jobs, applying for endless graduate schemes, slaving away as unpaid interns in the richest parts of the city, rolling confidently up to interviews with interviewers who turned them away as broken husks of humans. Polly laughed, and thought afresh of Hartlands, and the place that would be hers there.

It was in spite of the conversation at the Radisson that she did what Charles told her to do. The conversation was just talk; his words would fade and she would be left with Hartlands. It would be hers, uniquely hers, of that she was perfectly sure.

He had met her in the bar, just as he had promised her that he would. He was there already, sat at a little table in the corner, sipping whisky, no soda, it did not do to dilute the issue. He was dressed in a dinner jacket, and oozed a type of classical sophistication that elevated the rest of the room to make it seem polished and otherworldly.

He stood up when she arrived, of course, he was always the model of politeness. But instead of leaning in to kiss her cheek, he leant back and cocked his head, as if to take all of her in.

She was more than the perfect match for him that evening. She was dressed in a dusky red that gave some colour to her cheeks, and she had grazed her lips with a hint of scarlet lipstick. The dress clung loosely at her shoulders, and came in tightly at her waist, only to float back out again to settle just above her knees. There was a slight silver sparkle at her long white neck, which made her blue eyes glitter. Polly was undeniably beautiful during that conversation at the Radisson.

And he stood there, still cocking his head at her, his expression expressionless because she could not read him there, there at that moment.

Of course, going by that conversation at the Radisson, she should have just joined the others at the club. But it was precisely because the others were now at the club that she did not turn tail and run. The cool icy blue eyes that were staring back at her across the table in her finery would chase her as she fled across the bridge and above the delving weir. The dead leaden eyes of the streetlights would beam back out of the turbulent roll of the river, as it crashed along beneath her running feet. Tripping, tippling, metallic clashes would reverberate through her as she ran with velvet high heels away across the bridge. They would mock her, they would make her feel sad, bereft in this the icy heart of the mild summer's evening in June.

Empty and disconsolate, Polly's steps could only end back at the club, and she knew enough of devastation there to avoid it. She would catch some stranger's eye, and he would grab her and push her into the wall, or if she was lucky, the soft padded surround of the DJ booth. Maybe he would just have her there, there where everybody could see, but she could not see herself, back in that frosty mirror of her mind, speckled and dirty with dust, stained and fouled by lust.

"No," she breathed, sipping at a dirty Martini, because that was what he had ordered for her.

"No?" he repeated, his eyebrows twitching slightly as he leant back in his chair.

He paused, and knocked back the rest of the whisky in his glass. He clicked his fingers, the delicious affront, and summoned a waiter to the table.

"Another, please."

He held his steady stare at Polly, who was gazing down at the red velvet of her new high-heeled shoes.

"No?" he said again.

As she went into the La Senza store on Oxford Street, she heard a little voice saying no, and it must have been his voice saying no, in his irritating way, as all control was his, and his alone. She refused to think about that conversation, as she looked at the shop around her. The bright artificial colours of the neon lingerie around her made her blink. The pink bras and orange knickers, slung from the walls like strands of ivy on an acid trip, attacked her vision, angry aggressors in this the seedy world of human attraction and appetite.

"Can I help, madam?" a polite and nearly polished voice asked, with a whisper of something a little foreign in its tone.

The shop assistant had evidently identified Polly as a person of class.

"Can I help, madam? Is there anything in particular that you're looking for?"

Polly swung her gaze down onto the shop assistant, like a hungry bird of prey. But her glance was soft, and somewhat bemused, as she professed that she did not know.

But she did know, and she had told him what she wanted. She had said that she wanted to be able to feel.

"Feel what, Polly?"

She felt sure that he was mocking her. But then again, she couldn't really be certain about anything Charles Caraway said.

"I don't know. People talk a lot about feelings, and I suppose I don't understand them all that much."

"I know you don't understand them."

"I'm getting married," Polly told the shop assistant.

The shop assistant smiled indulgently. Here was another happy bride-to-be. Bryan had proposed a month ago, and soon she would be buying little bits here and there, nothing too extravagant. It was only going to be a simple wedding, with the reception down at the local pub, but she wanted to please him that way, all the same. It was only what he deserved.

She led Polly towards the back of the shop, away from the acidic neons and the black corsets with bright red ribbons. Here, all was white.

"But you don't know how to feel, do you Polly?"

Then Polly remembered, she had confided in him that one time, the very first time, when they had met in the café and she was surprised to hear herself talk like that. Perhaps she had said something like that, that she was not able to feel. But that was before she had seen Hartlands. Everything had changed after she had seen Hartlands.

"Which one do you like?"

All the bras were white and frilly and lacy. They did not seem very different to Polly.

"I'm only an A cup," Polly said, placing her fingers abstractedly over the lace, feeling but not feeling all the same.

"Perhaps you need to learn how to feel," Charles had suggested, as he leant back once more, flicking his eyes over every inch of Polly's body, monitoring her every reaction. "What do you feel?"

"There are things we can do about that, padding is very wonderful, yes?"

The shop assistant passed her a bra. It felt remarkably heavy in Polly's pale hands.

"It will make you a C now. And without surgery, too. A very good buy."

"There are things I do feel," Polly insisted, some colour winding its way into her cheeks.

Perhaps the dirty Martini had gone to her head. Polly the teetotal was running behind her, ready to catch her up, all the while smiling a knowing smile.

"Do you like it? And there are the knickers that match, here."

The shop assistant placed a white thong into Polly's hands, and she shuddered.

"No, not like that."

"What do you feel, then?" he had insisted.

He sounded like he did not believe her, but he was probably just playing games. It was only a bit of conversation at the Radisson, and it surely did not mean much, if anything at all.

"I prefer something a bit more classic," Polly stuttered out, returning the thong to where it hung.

"Classically sexy," the shop assistant nodded knowingly, and found an alternative pair of more substantial white lacy knickers.

"I feel, well, sometimes when I close my eyes," and Polly closed her eyes, sat there at the Radisson, and Charles disappeared, and she was there again, spinning round, the whole world a blur. "I'm back at the club with the others. It spins, it whirls, the lights hurt me, and all I can smell is sweat, and vomit, so mixed together I can't tell one from the other. And now the drink I'm drinking, it's probably water, but it tastes like vomit too. I smell of it, it's like I'm part of it, and I'm afraid that I won't ever be able to get out of it."

"Does madam require anything else? Our bridal suspenders and corset are very popular too."

Polly shook her head, and gripped the white lacy lingerie tightly together in her hands.

"What is that, though, Polly? You can't base your relationship with the feeling world on some sordid student nightclub. It just doesn't work like that."

He was laughing, but it was horrid laughter, hollow and forced, she could not join in with it. She had expressed how she felt, but according to him those feelings were not valid, not acceptable currency, in his world at Hartlands.

The shop assistant took Polly to the till. She was slightly disappointed. She had spent a long time with this woman, who did not seem to appreciate the attention. Oh yes, the lady was very beautiful, with a figure most women would kill for, but there was something odd about her that she could not quite put her finger on. Perhaps she was not quite all there, it was possible. Perhaps she had made this husband up? The shop assistant had heard of such things. But she put the items through the till, and smiled radiantly back at Polly.

"I'm sorry, I don't understand."

Polly shook her head, weakly, pushing back the dirty Martini so it glided a little way across the marble surface of the table towards him. A merry group, another student and her family, laughed hysterically behind them.

"All right then, Polly, we'll try it like this. Now, tell me about pleasure. What precisely is pleasure?"

They had only given her a little bag from La Senza. She now had to find the dress. She did not have much of a budget, and she would have to search for it on the high street. Before, back before she had met Charles Carraway, she had always thought that she would go to the little bridal boutique in the neighbouring town. She saw the shop now, vaguely, as if it was shrouded in the mists somewhere along Oxford Street.

Polly struck out along Oxford Street, hardly knowing where she was going. But then she remembered that she had heard of Monsoon doing a nice little range of wedding dresses. She would head there, and see what the shop had to offer her.

"Pleasure, I think pleasure is release," Polly mused, as if rendered idle by Charles' question.

Meanwhile she had refrained from fidgeting, although she kept her gaze ticking between the contemplation of her martini glass and her shoes. She would have to steady herself if she was going to master those intellectual playing fields that Charles so relished.

Oxford Street was busy. Around her, numerous Spanish tourists spoke in quick and incoherent babbles. Then there were the young, the beautifully dressed in Topshop, resplendent with their own vintage twist, long and lean like Polly, but unlike her they were decidedly of the age, of the fashion, belonging to this century rather than the last. There were more tourists: Germans, probably, and

Americans, complete with bum bags. Polly didn't think they made bum bags any more. She waded up the street. She wanted to falter, she wanted to scream. She felt trapped, but she was getting married in three days, and she had to find a dress before it was too late.

"Release into the cold night air," she continued, looking from Charles out through the glass facade of the Radisson, to the streetlights outside, and the river beating lazily around its generous meander.

"And your white sheets, all clean, and smelling like Fairy," Charles nodded, as if he knew it all.

Polly now stood in front of a collection of white dresses. There were no shop assistants around her this time. She was free to choose for herself. She thought that she would be deadened by the white; he had said something about the white during that conversation at the Radisson, but she was surprised, because she was immediately drawn to one particular dress. It was full length, with an empire line, covered by a layer of lace, which was embellished by little stars of silver. He hadn't of course liked the silver round her neck at the Radisson. It had devalued her own special beauty.

"Because it's from Accessorize? And not Chanel?"

It had been his opening gambit in their conversation, and she had replied with spirit. But he had immediately changed the subject, elusive tonight, a fragment of gold glittering beneath the river mud, the waters flooding up over it. She could wait until the tide flowed out, desperate to find it and seize it, this beautiful, rare thing, but she would find that it was already gone, vanished, covered up by the river slime.

Polly stood in the changing room. She knew she should have a doting mother with her, but she was telling her mother only when she was safely tucked away on her honeymoon in Spain, where Charles kept a villa. Her mother could not hurt her there.

She took off her clothes, the long safari-toned skirt, the belt, and the white blouse, and stood in her underwear, trying not to catch the gaze of her own eyes in the mirror. They had changed, they sparkled, and they frightened her.

She wondered how on earth she was going to get the dress on without any help. She did not want to be gawped over by some sympathetic shop assistant, and she felt with some shame that she was a pitiful spectacle, her the lonely bride. But assistance was a necessary evil, and so she rang the little bell for some help.

"Everyone can feel that, Polly. I hate to spoil the illusion, but your mind is hardly special. Your body, on the other hand."

He paused and leant forward, grinning. Then he abruptly retreated to his former position, finishing his drink with a lurid, violent, flourish.

Polly sipped at her dirty Martini, and said nothing.

As it happened the shop assistant was very kind, and not overbearing in her kindness. She had seen a situation like this before, at her previous job at a little boutique. A quick wedding, low key, no family; she tried not to pity this bride-to-be stood in front of her, who looked so fragile in the long white dress. For Polly did not know it, but the dress had softened her and feminised her angles, transforming her into something delicate and ethereal.

"Would you like a veil to go with it?"

"Polly, I'll get to the point," Charles said, placing his glass back down upon the table with a jolt.

Polly, wishing that he would, jumped at the noise and stared impassively back at him.

"You don't know how to feel."

19

"I suppose so," Polly gulped.

She was still staring at herself, the image reflecting back at her, this woman as a girl bride. She imperceptibly tugged at the strange material clinging to her thin frame, just to check that it was real, and not the fabric of some outrageous dream.

The shop assistant left her to go and search the stockroom for the matching veil. Polly stood still, perfectly still, and waited.

"You can be awfully patronising sometimes," Polly drawled.

She could not tell whether this was the beginning or the end of the conversation.

"You need a patron," Charles said, and his face relaxed into a proper smile for the first time that evening.

The rowdy party got up behind them. They were all going to the club, parents included. This one night of graduation, you could flick back the clock and suddenly be young again, and sip at the vodka-flavoured fountain of eternal youth.

It was between five and seven minutes when the shop assistant returned with profuse apologies. She was new to the store, and was having trouble locating things. Polly dismissed the apology with a wave of her hand, murmuring how it didn't matter, it just didn't matter.

She took the veil from the girl's hand, and brought it up to her black hair. She closed her eyes, and the shop girl exhaled in astonishment. Now here was really a thing of beauty.

"I am my own person," Polly replied, in that level way, which spoke not of angry impertinence, but was the natural flow that stemmed from her own reasonableness. Surely reason was the only weapon with which she could take on Professor Charles Carraway?

"But we're marrying, you and I, and that will end."

"Such a fairy-tale dress, madam, I hope you get your fairy-tale ending," the shop assistant commented, charmed.

She was captivated. Polly had provoked in her a joyous sense that she was partaking in something splendid, from which only happiness could pour. And Polly did look truly the princess, there, in that changing room, which tried to be chic like some gorgeous Parisian boudoir, with its great purple curtains and its outlandish flowered wallpaper.

"You won't ever do anything, you know, Polly," he said.

"Is this conversation over now?" Polly asked, quite politely given the situation.

"Four hundred and ninety pounds seventy-five please, ain't they lovely, that dress and that veil?"

It was a different girl at the till, but she too was captivated.

"When's the big day?"

"Never," Charles shook his head wryly, the old fox in him alive still. "Stay, I'll get you another drink."

Polly left the shop and felt curiously empty, although she was now weighted down by the shopping bags. She knew other brides-to-be had the flowers to sort out, the favours to make, and the bridesmaids to assemble. She should really be now grappling with the seating plan, deciding what to do with her stepmother and her despised half-sister, and whether or not to sit her divorced parents together.

She dismissed it, and wiped away the thoughts of what might have been. She knew the way it was going to be, because Charles had been so kind as to tell her everything. Polly was going into this marriage with her eyes wide open, and she was glad, yes, she told herself that she was glad.

CHAPTER TWO

The first Polly's mother heard of any wedding was in mid July. She had been sat outside enjoying the rare good weather in her small courtyard garden, which she had filled with a fountain and a fish pond, and a few pots of geraniums. She liked to think that she was in Spain, or Italy, or some such other exotic place, instead of the provincial English market town she called home.

She had been rather riled when the telephone rang, although most things riled Polly's mother. But she was riled today because it was lunchtime, the sun was at its warmest, and so she did not want to leave her beautiful garden.

She softened when she saw that Polly was calling. The girl had gone off on a last-minute package deal somewhere hot with some of her girl friends from university, and Moira was glad that Polly was at last exhibiting some of the usual traits of the youth she seemed to have negated during her childhood and subsequent adolescence. But soon the holiday would come to an end, and the girl would have to set about finding some work. Polly had never worked before, but that was a small matter, and now, thankfully, she seemed to have forgotten all about that odious Charles Carraway and his untold wealth.

Charles Carraway had undoubtedly been a moment of rebellious madness on her daughter's part. It was an infatuation that had started in a local coffee shop, something about Polly answering an advertisement he had placed, back in the Easter holidays. Thankfully, Polly had returned to university, and Charles Caraway was gone, forgotten, yesterday's news, although Moira could not quite forgive him for spoiling the innocence of her youngest daughter. Men like that should be locked up, and the key thrown away.

The line was crackling, fizzing up a storm. Moira had to strain her battered hearing to make out what Polly was saying. Something about Spain. Something about Charles Carraway. Something about being married.

Of course Moira had blown up purple and in her rage had spat down the telephone such expletives and angry words that Polly had eventually hung up, cowed and ashamed, or so her mother in her self-righteousness had assumed.

From then on things were not right with Moira Andrews. Her health fell into a decline. Shingles followed on from a long cough she could not rid herself of, and she had to give up her part-time job at a local antiques market. Her friends privately conjectured that her daughter had broken her heart, but all that was wrong with Moira was her stubbornness. She had not wanted Polly to marry Charles Carraway, and she could not forgive Polly for erring against her better judgement. For all intents and purposes, her daughter was dead to her. And so Moira's fit of piqued colic lasted for many months, weathering even another phone call from Polly once she had arrived back in England and tried to broker a tentative peace deal.

Moria would not see her. Moira would not have anything at all to do with her. And Moira was made of such determined mettle that she did not succumb to her protective maternal instinct for some time, knowing as she did that Polly was holed up at Charles Carraway's stately home all alone, without any means of transport, vulnerable, poor child that she was. She shelved away her fears, stacking them underneath her other concerns, those for her health, and those for her eldest, most precious, daughter, Petunia.

But Moira was not built so entirely without love to forget her youngest daughter so very completely. The archived fears gradually assembled themselves into something like a whisper, getting at her in the night, and when she woke up in the morning. And then the whisper got louder until it neared a shout. Life was short, of that she was all too aware, and she realised with a stab of guilty pain that she had neglected her younger daughter for far too long.

She could not ignore the lull of her maternal instinct for much longer. Fed up of being shrouded by bridge nights and aborted attempts at ballroom dancing, it crashed into her consciousness when several months had gone by, when summer had most decidedly faded into winter, and it was by now November.

It was then that Moira decided to call Polly. She dialled the number, and waited, not without some anxiety. What if Polly should shun her? What then? Moira's pride would not allow her to try and bury the hatchet one more time. There could only be one peace mission, and this was it.

But Polly's phone was off, and without a voicemail. Moira did not at first know whether she felt relief, gratitude that a most likely difficult conversation had been eschewed, but then as she tried calling again at intervals throughout the day, she began to feel guilty for having felt so relieved. What had happened to Polly? Where might she be? It was criminal for that girl to be left alone at that big old house without any means of communication.

Moira's fears rose into an agitated howling much like the neighbour's dog set up most nights when it wanted its dinner. Before she quite knew what she was doing she had donned her mac and had got into her old Volvo and was steaming out of Petworth heading west, on the trail of Charles Carraway and his new bride.

Moira did not know much about Charles Carraway, and nor did the local gossips of her acquaintance. That being said, they remembered him from the old days, of say, twenty years ago, his glamorous wife and their endless parties. But it was thought that he had abandoned the place, and severed all ties, since she had left him and taken his son away. It was a crying shame, but now Charles Carraway passed unnoticed under the radar, a forgotten memento of those heady days of the eighties, when glamour was impossible and greed was infinite.

But Moira did know that Charles Carraway lived at a large stately pile, which was not far distant from her own home. She knew it could be accessed by turning right off the main drag, but where that road could be found, she was not as enlightened. After taking several wrong turns, and ending up in farmyards and at dead ends, she was about to give up. In one last final effort, however, she pulled up in an entrance to a field, and rummaged around in the glove compartment in the hopes of finding an old map, which she had used to ferry her eldest daughter around to various pony clubs across the county.

Moira was startled by a loud hammering on the window of her car. She looked up to see a woman about the same age as herself, dressed in a short wax jacket and sensible waterproof trousers, gesturing for her to wind the window down.

"I say, are you lost?"

"I'm looking for Charles Carraway's house," Moira replied, once she had collected herself.

She was astute enough to notice that a cloud passed across the good Samaritan's face.

"This field separates Hartlands, which is what his house is called, from the road. Here, get out of the car and you'll get a better idea."

Moira obeyed the stranger. Exiting the car, she was struck by a fresh north-easterly breeze, which played havoc with her short bob of black hair. She nodded as she listened to the directions, back down the road, second left, beside the old tumbledown lodge.

"I'm one to speak plainly," her saviour began, in those strident plummy tones that assaulted Moira with a whiff of perfect breeding, "you know Charles Carraway then? He's not often back down here, he prefers the London life by all accounts."

Moira hesitated, and then nodded.

"There are rumours going around that he's married again. But I don't believe them myself. It was what one calls a traumatic divorce he had, and what with the son being spirited away to Argentina by his mother, how is a man meant to get over that? And you would think that if he had married again, that she would be out and about the place, you know, helping with the Harvest supper night, going about with the hunt, helping with our fundraising campaign. Have you seen our church tower? It's such a beauty, Turner painted it you know, and really that Carraway should do more to help us out. He's as rich as Croesus, by all accounts. But what I'm saying is that it's the way of things, you see, it's what old Mrs Carraway used to do, not the South American one, the mother."

Moira nodded.

"Oh, I see you must be getting on. Remember, it's second on the left, and usually the gate there is closed. See if you can open it though, and then follow the drive right along the top of the valley until you reach the house, you won't be able to miss it. Now, where has my bloody dog got to? Sasha! Sasha, come here girl!"

Exhausted by her monologue, the lady in the wax jacket drew out a much maligned dog whistle and blew hard on it. Presently, Sasha came bounding up, a big, glossy and healthy looking black Labrador, who nearly knocked Moira over in her exuberance to return to her mistress. Moira, not a dog lover by any stretch of the imagination, bent down to pat her.

"Oh, I wouldn't do that. She's meant to be a gun dog, and shouldn't be petted and clucked over. It's just not the way we do things, is it, Sasha?"

Sasha panted by way of reply, and then she and her owner had gone, as quickly as they had appeared, striding up the lane at an alarmingly fast pace.

Moira got back into the car, feeling as though she had been winded by the onslaught of information. But it only confirmed what she had suspected, and she again wondered whether she was on a fool's errand, that perhaps Polly was in London, doing her Masters as she had always wished to do.

Empty and deflated, she followed her directions to the letter. Without any difficulty, she found the ancient cottage that purported to be some kind of lodge house, and got out of her car to open the gate. It was then that she noticed the old cattle grid, and with a grim expression she fell to prising apart the worn latch, knowing full well that the Volvo's suspension was not equal to the journey she had to now make.

With hands covered in rusty grime from the gate, Moira got back into her car and bumped across the cattle grid. She was so preoccupied with the business of then closing the gate, wiping her hands clean, and setting the car into motion once more, that she did not notice the female figure who was rounding the bend in front of her. Dressed in a large green Barbour jacket, her frail little frame was smothered, weakened, pressed down into the muddy earth below as she advanced down along the overgrown track.

Moira did not recognise her at first. She had mistaken her for some other walker, another Sasha-owning type. There was nothing familiar about the figure she passed, except when she considered how dark her hair was, and how pale she looked. That particular hair colour was her own, and that particular skin colour belonged to her also. That female figure in the green coat was her own flesh and blood, and overcome by her joy at the impending reunion between mother and daughter, Moira screeched the old car into reverse and began to chase Polly backwards down the drive.

Wildly, the woman swung round, and Moira saw that she had been right, that it was her daughter that she had passed. But Polly had shrunk, she was somehow shrivelled like an elderly woman who has gone off her food. She was thinner, if that was even possible, for she had only ever been a skeleton with cheekbones. Her blue eyes were wide, and filled with impossible tears. Polly never cried. But now teardrops streamed down her cheeks, and stuck to her bright red flesh, as she choked and heaved, trying desperately to hold them back.

"What are you doing?" she asked, in a shrill, high voice, a demented voice that went straight through her mother. "What are you doing here?"

"I've come to see you, Polly," Moira said, quite gently considering how gentleness was not part of her usual armoury, "it's been too long."

She had got out of the car and had advanced down the drive a couple of metres, arms outstretched and ready to take her daughter into her arms for an overdue hug, a hug for which Polly had been waiting since she was a little girl. But Polly hung back, her face crumbling.

"Come on Polly, I won't bite. I'm your mother."

"You shouldn't have come."

Moira at this point thought that Polly had suffered some sort of matrimonial dispute. Heaven knew how many of those she had suffered during the course of her short marriage to Geoffrey Andrews, and this was what tied her sympathy even further to her tear-ravaged daughter.

"Get into the car, Polly, and I'll drive you back up to the house. We'll have a nice cup of tea, eh?"

Polly was by now too weak to resist, and she got back into the car, which Moira drove back towards Hartlands. All the way up the long winding drive that skirted the green valley Polly was silent.

"We'll go this way, through the kitchen, it's better," she finally said, once her mother had parked the car outside the big old house that looked ominous in the winter light.

Moira shivered, and followed her daughter, who neglected to explain how Charles resented that she preferred to use the little servants' door instead of the grand entrance hall, which was now shut up and encaged by mothballs. The servants' door was hidden amongst the ivy, sat on the north wing, and it led down into the bowels of the house, the great big kitchen that Charles had done up several years ago, with its wheezing old AGA belching out heat, and the fine old Dorset flagstones gracing the floor as the oak chairs grazed across it.

There was a lot of screeching from the aforementioned flagstones as Polly pulled out a chair for her mother and instructed her to take a seat. Moira remained unusually silent, struggling to formulate her thoughts.

The kettle screamed into life and Polly rubbed her hands by the AGA. This was Hartlands, it was her domain, and he had told her that this was the way it was going to be, five months ago at the Radisson.

"It's the house, isn't it Polly, it's the house?" he demanded, although she wondered why he even had to ask.

It was as if he had chucked her up by the chin, standing so close to her that she could feel his breath on her cheek. She felt as if he had started to rub his hands down her body, feeling the soft folds of that dusky red dress and what lay beneath it, her flesh, still and quiet and not quite able to respond to his touch.

"It's okay, it grabs you like that."

He should have been grabbing her, seizing her at the small of her back, pulling his lips in tight against the cool curve of her neck.

"It happens, it happens like that."

He should have been lifting up the hem of her dress, tracing his fingers along the inside of her thigh. But instead he sat across from her, the sphinx, the marble table between them, and smiled, his matinee idol smile fresh from another century.

Polly sat down opposite her mother. Her mother was not a sensitive woman, nor was she predisposed to any great outpourings of feeling. But even she could tell that Polly was lost to her. She was not the daughter she had known. And she watched, concerned, but curious like the woman before her had no prior claims on her affection, no ties to her blood, a stranger in this strange kitchen, as Polly's eyes ran red, red and sore and hollow.

"So you know we married, I think I told you that," Polly began, placing her shaking hands down on the table, the cold band of gold on her finger rattling slightly as she did so.

"It happens like that in marriage, that both partners have their separate roles. I'm the academic, as you can see. I've written books, I give a lot of lectures, and there's the name of professor on my card. I've arrived. But what about you, Polly, what about you?"

Polly looked at him.

"I'm in need of my perfect setting?"

"My words. Use yours."

"It was at the town hall in Islington. We got witnesses off the street and paid them twenty pounds. I believe they thought that it was quite romantic, or maybe that I was marrying him so I could get a green card. The old lady was nice though, and cried. I didn't cry. I didn't even have any flowers, because Charles said they would tarnish my special beauty."

Polly's voice cracked with a perceptible hint of bitterness, but she rallied, faltering only very slightly.

"I've got some photos, somewhere, I think I got the other witness to take them on my phone. He was the gentleman-tramp type, at least I think that's what you call them. I got the photos for you Mum, I thought you'd like to see me in my wedding dress."

Polly trailed off, a wistful smile spreading across her face. Meanwhile the artificial heat of the kitchen had all but eradicated the wild glow of her cheeks that her mother had collided with on the drive. She was back to the cold old Polly she knew, with her enviably smooth pale skin. But something had changed about her daughter, and Moira shivered again as she noticed it. Her cheeks, although still cold and smooth, were somehow also ghastly and hollow. If she peered at her closely enough, she could see the edges of her cheekbones sat there right next to her skin. It was like she was staring at the skull starring in a production of *Hamlet*.

Disturbed and in desperate need of a distraction, Moira looked around for any sign of Polly's phone. She would like to have seen the photographs, and was moved more than she knew that Polly had, after all, thought of her on her wedding day. Perhaps if she could find the phone and its photographs they could be more like mother and daughter again.

"Hartlands," Polly began, stirring the olive in her dirty Martini with a cocktail stick, "Hartlands is my role."

"It's still my word."

"It's your house," Polly replied, unblinkingly.

"But how can the house be your role? What does it even mean?"

Polly explained to her mother that she no longer had a phone.

"We don't get signal here. The valley creates a strange dipped effect, and so it's a notorious black spot for phone signal."

Polly smiled, those were Charles' words, and she regurgitated them with a peculiar pleasure.

"So there's no point really, as I'm always in the house. I'm the house's keeper, and the house keeps me."

"Hartlands will keep you, you know, Polly."

Charles had answered his own question because Polly had remained stubbornly silent, staring at her martini glass.

"I don't mind, it's so pretty," she replied, without any obstinacy.

She looked down at her delicate little watch. It was well past eleven, and she would not get into the club easily now, and she began to wonder whether it was worth going there at all. She imagined the long queue snaking up the cobbles, the broken glass gleaming as it crunched under the sharp heels of the young girls ready and waiting for the most perfect night of them all, this the very last one. Everybody would be there. But there was no point going now.

She looked around her and was surprised that the bar at the Radisson was still open at this late hour. Parents sat around, drinking with and without their children. It was a special night, and they would converse on, regardless of whether Polly went to the club, or if she went home desolate in her dusky red dress.

"It's very pretty," Moira began, breaking the silence that had ensued, as she looked around the kitchen and fought for something, anything, to say.

Polly was staring down at her hands, minutely examining the gold ring, which shone back her reflection with surprising clarity. She lifted a hand to touch her cheeks, to feel if the bones were really so pronounced, and flinched in a moment of fright and panic, thinking that it was Charles who had touched her instead. Her chair screeched against the flagstones as she leapt up and span around, until she finally came to a rest leaning against one of the work surfaces.

"Polly, it's all right," Moira purred, trying to sooth her daughter, placing an arm around her as she did so.

Polly drew up rigid, and shuddered Moira's hand off her shoulders.

"Your role can be Hartlands, because you've chosen it, haven't you?"

Polly no longer wanted to listen. She thought of the club and the howling din of music, and felt torn. She began to not want to be there at the Radisson. Charles had pushed this conversation too far, and she was beginning to feel unsettled.

"And you, Charles, I choose you," she said, stirring herself from her languid position, leaning on the back of her chair.

"Do you really, Polly, do you really?"

33

She put down the martini glass and grasped his hands, and held them firmly in her own this time.

"Is it a test? Is it a game? Of course I want you."

"Oh Polly, shall we have another drink? Let's."

CHAPTER THREE

Polly was sat on the bed at Charles Carraway's London bolt-hole, a horrible little flat with one bedroom and dirty kitchen that the academic divorcee, or newlywed as he was now, never saw fit to clean. He hadn't even bothered to clean it for his new bride, whom he had taken by the hand up the stairs of this trendy Islington townhouse until they had reached the top, his attic, his haunt, his lair.

She was still wearing her wedding dress. The bedcover beneath her was a putrid yellow, salvaged from one of the old servant's bedrooms at Hartlands, and the rancid colour seeped into the pure white of her girlish wedding gown. Polly now looked like the bride who had gone off, like sour milk.

He had given her a glass of wine, red wine, and said that he didn't have any champagne. A week ago, at graduation, she could have had all the champagne she wanted. But here, on her wedding night, she sat on the bed, holding a glass of wine that affronted her in its cheapness. And Charles Carraway had gone, but Polly wasn't sure where to.

She had vague memories from their conversation at the Radisson about the wedding night. Of course she was expecting that he would sleep with her. That was what the gentlemanly type of tramp had not so gentlemanly suggested: here was Polly, at the peak of her youth and her beauty, ripe and ready for the plucking.

"You'll be there for Hartlands, and all its needs."

"And your needs too."

She had smiled, deeply, down through her eyelashes and back up at him. Polly never spoke in innuendo, but here she was, making a decent start at it.

"Of course," he said, somewhat dismissively.

Of course. It had rattled down her spine. She took a sip of the disgusting wine to try and calm her. She knew it was going to hurt, and maybe the dark red liquid would numb the pain.

Polly was actually beginning to feel quite discomposed, a sensation with which she was not well acquainted. The wedding itself had not scared her; she didn't even feel like she'd been there. The woman in the mirror who had been wearing her dress had been there instead, the fairy-tale princess, was that what the sales assistant had called her? The fairy-tale princess married to her prince.

She heard the door bang. He must have come back. Perhaps he had brought some champagne with him.

"I don't live outrageously, I don't dine on oysters. Excess has no appeal to me, but I eat and drink what I like, and occasionally pick up nice things at auction," he had explained, back at the Radisson, at the start or the end of the conversation, she did not recall.

Charles came into the room, but he didn't have anything in his hands. He did not explain where he had been, and so he stood, staring down at Polly in her yellow-white dress, her new wedding band, and her fingers wrapped around the edge of the wine glass.

Earlier, they had been out to dinner, at least it wasn't at some ghastly chain restaurant, and now the clock was ticking on to half past nine in the evening. Still light outside, the garish London heat was forcing its way through the windows, mingling with the stale bookish smell that pervaded the entire flat. It was hardly the atmosphere for heady pleasure, but Charles continued to look down at his new bride.

"Pleasure is, pleasure is feeling, feeling those real sensations Polly, those sensations you can't ever expect, that aren't manufactured. Like when you go for a walk, a walk in winter. You've layered up magnificently on your top half with jumper after jumper, but your jeans don't keep your legs warm enough. So the cold pricks, tickles, at your thighs, and it's the strangest, most exhilarating, feeling."

Polly confessed that it sounded a more interesting pleasure than the clammy relief of stepping outside of the club in the early hours of the morning; relief that the boys around her no longer saw her as fair game, that now she could put at least one of her housemates to bed and know she would be safe that night. But then again, that was a feeling that she could not expect Charles Carraway to reasonably understand.

Polly stood up from the bed, and saying nothing, she stepped across the little scrap of floor that separated her from her new husband. Mrs Polly Carraway, of Hartlands, it sounded well, if not somewhat fey and wistful.

As she stood up from the bed, the strange yellow glow having fled from her, she was like a long tall fairy, a dint of magic flying at the edges of her eyes. Charles stepped back, almost instinctively, and banged his head on the ceiling, which sloped down above him into the eaves.

He swore, and he hardly ever swore. In fact, it was the first time she had ever heard him lapse into bad language.

She put a quiet hand out to stroke the back of his neck. This she had seen her friends do many times when they wished to secure the attention of the opposite sex. Letting the fingers of her right hand caress their way through the roots of his thick but greying hair, she brought up her other hand to touch his neck, pressing her lips up to his chin.

For a glorious moment, he gave into her, kissing her back enthusiastically, letting his hands run down her body, until he picked her up, and tossed her onto the bed. But he didn't continue to kiss her as she expected, or try to undo the dress, which she had recruited a lady to do up for her in the murky depths of the toilets at Victoria Station.

"I married you to look at Polly, not to touch."

It was crushing, and then he left the room.

"You see Polly, you shouldn't really be touched. When I asked you about pleasure, you didn't know, you couldn't explain it. We're both adult enough to know what type of pleasure most people enjoy. And I like that about you Polly, I really do. Yours isn't a seedy beauty, I don't wish to ravage you. I just want to enjoy you, to cherish you, as something really, truly, precious. That's why you'll love Hartlands, a jewel returning to its proper setting. It's late, and I can't think of a better metaphor. But that's what you'll be, Polly, a jewel returning to its proper setting."

He had spoken the truth. It was late. The people around them were getting up, retiring, heading to the lifts at the other side of the room. Polly heard their clinks and chimes like they were a million miles away, ghostly and distant. She didn't have the energy to argue with him any more. Besides, he had called her precious, and she had never really been precious to anybody before. He was going to cherish her, and not plunge her back down into the pillows to take his pleasure from her.

Polly was lying on her pillows now, somewhat dazed. She reached out for the wine, perilously positioned on the willow table beside the bed. It perched on a thin Henry James novella, *Daisy Miller*, but Polly did not want to read. He had touched her. Yet he had not touched her. He did not want to touch her. She was confused, and thought she should have paid better attention to their conversation, a week ago, at the Radisson. She drank more of the wine, and reflected that there had been a time once when she did not want to be touched.

She got up from the bed with some difficulty. The dress was tight against her skin, and it restricted her movement. The heavy wires of the white lacy bra dug into her; it was not a good fit. She knew that she could not get out of the dress without help, so she went to the door, and pushed it open.

Charles sat in the next room, flicking through the television channels, the hysteria of game shows mingling with the subdued tones of a nature programme. He sat in his shirt, undone at the neck, and his heavy black suit trousers.

Polly sloped round the edge of the door. She did not smile, but gave him her level stare, without any hint of judgement or reproach in her blue eyes. The floorboards creaked as she slowly advanced across the room, but he did not look up.

"Charles," she cooed, surprised at this voice that vibrated like a gentle melody from between her parted lips, "Charles."

He looked up.

"I will prize you, you know, Polly, and treat you as you ought to be treated. This is love, Polly, in its purest form. I will protect you, guard you, prize you, Polly. You need not worry for anything, and I've already begun seeing to that."

He said goodbye later, and then she left the Radisson. It was gone midnight, and she decided to go to bed.

"What is it?"

He kept his attention on the television, flicking through the channels. Now he was watching the news. Someone had been murdered, or kidnapped, or something like that. Polly felt a little butterfly throbbing in her stomach. She did not know how to handle the situation, and most of all, how she could handle him.

"Guide you, Polly, I will guide you to perfection."

He hadn't spoken. It was the remnants of the conversation at the Radisson that hung about her like the offensive odour of rotting flesh.

"I need some help."

Polly slowly turned around to reveal the back of her dress, the buttons that stretched down along her back to the top of her thighs.

"Whatever for?"

The presenter was now talking about the weather. The heatwave was set to continue.

"I can't undo it by myself, Charles."

"How did you get into it, then?"

He robbed his eyes from the television and stole a look at her, her long neck winding round to gaze at him, her fingers on the back of the dress illustrating how she was trapped within its delicate lace, like a fly trapped in the flimsy twine of an ornate spider's web, wriggling to be set free. He turned his eyes back towards the screen. He could not bear her in his sight, as she strained to be let out of her dress.

"A woman in the toilets at Victoria Station. I gave her five pounds to help me."

Charles shook his head, disbelieving.

"I didn't need to know that. I only needed to see the result, you standing there at the town hall, tall and elegant and so wonderfully poised. I didn't need to know about the grubby woman in the toilets."

"I never said she was grubby."

"Why did she take the money, then? Grasping opportunism is hardly the purest of motives for charity."

"I need to be let out of this dress, Charles, I can't stay in it forever."

He stood up, slowly. She shivered as she remembered his words, and she did not expect for him to touch her. So she shivered again as he placed his hands around her back, her standing in front of him, facing the other way, looking into the squalid little bedroom with its queen-sized bed.

"Was that a shiver or a shudder, Polly?" he asked, the words caressing, demanding at her neck, as he bent down to her, his hands gradually moving down, down, till he could feel the slight curve of her hips.

He now begun to undo the buttons, one by one, starting from the top. When he reached the sight of her bra, he paused, and with a quick flick that surprised her, undid it. He carried on undoing the buttons. It felt like ten minutes until he had undone them all.

When he had finished, Polly stepped away, obediently, ready to find some sort of shroud to hide herself in. But then, she suddenly found herself naked, exposed, the dress had come off all around her, and lay on the dusty wooden floor, fodder for Miss Havisham.

It was a mean trick. He had placed his foot on the slight train of the dress, and when she walked away, the dress had come tumbling down around her.

She turned, confused, to face him, covering herself with her long pale arms. Charles curled his lips into a smile, and sat back down.

Polly ran back into the bedroom to retrieve her dressing gown, and came back in, switching off the television as she did so.

"What sort of man have I married?" she demanded, her voice cracking, full of exasperated horror.

"My darling Polly, did our conversation at the Radisson not show you the type of man I am, rather than the type of man I appear to be?"

Not that conversation at the Radisson. It was ridiculous to her now. It was dirty Martinis and his intellect fighting hers across the low marble table. It was the people laughing around her, and the river crashing away outside. It was the dial of her watch and its hands as they ticked, and all the while her imagination was vivid with the picture of the club oscillating round and round. It was a play act, a test of her nerve, civilised conversation pushed to the extreme. It was him showing off, demonstrating how he should be played. And above all, it was what she had to endure, if she was to step a little closer to Hartlands.

Polly shivered, which was bizarre because it was July. They were at the top of a big building, in a room with sloping attic windows facing south-west, boiling and broiling in the summer heat. They were covered by the choke of the exhaust fumes, and the gloat of the sirens. Polly shivered again.

"I don't really remember all of it, we were there for hours."

"It was two hours, Polly, don't exaggerate. Come here, and sit next next to me."

He gestured to the space beside him on the grubby sofa. It was some nineteen seventies nightmare, a vision in green and velveteen, pockmarked by cigarette burns. It seemed familiar. It was like something out of her student house back at university. The irony dug into Polly like a branding iron, sizzling the pricking hairs on her skin.

But she did as she was told, this frail little thing, bound together in her flimsy white silk dressing gown. It was inadequate, and hardly covered her. When she sat down, he could see right up to the top of her thighs, where the white frilly lace of the knickers she had bought, just three days ago, nestled.

"I am the man you married, Charles Carraway, out of your will and your better judgement. I've scared you, haven't I? Perhaps you'll try and diagnose me with the second-hand psychology all you English students seem to relish. But don't bother, you won't get anywhere with it. Maybe I'm a misogynist? Or a misanthrope? Which do you think sounds better? But that still won't get you anywhere, will it?"

Polly shook her head, although why she did so, she did not quite understand. She stared at the television's blank black screen, rubbing her fingers on the cord of her dressing gown. She knew there was an exit, just behind them on the sofa, back out and down the stairs. She could run. Nobody knew they were married. There was no shame in it, divorced at twenty-one. It could have been a blip, and maybe they could just separate. She would keep the name, though, she liked the name. It made her different to the Polly that she had been before.

"I plainly stated the terms and conditions to this marriage."

Polly strove with the heat now, as a waft of humid air fluttered in through the open window and pushed the blinds apart, bringing a buzzing bluebottle in with it.

"You'll be there for Hartlands, and you'll be there for me. You won't want for anything, then. What's money, when you have a house like that? What's society to you, when you're framed so delightfully in a glorious house like Hartlands? You'll be beautiful, my dear, I promise. Really, truly, my darling, do you need anything else?"

Polly relapsed to stirring her dirty Martini with the cocktail stick, vulnerable in the misty green waters of the drink that shocked her every time she took a sip. She nodded her acknowledgement, thinking of the house, and that thought enough was glorious.

"Do I really have to remind you?" Charles drawled, laying a sweaty hand on Polly's thigh, and holding it there.

He did not squeeze or caress her, but he simply held his hand there prone, waiting. Meanwhile Polly shook her head again, and turned to face him with her eyes wide open.

"I think I am to understand that I am to have no allowance from you. I think I am to understand that I am to expect no company, no friends, especially none of my acquaintances from university. Think of how they degrade me!"

She had almost scoffed at him as she bitterly redelivered to him his words, albeit it dressed up in a different envelope. But she controlled the wobbling of her voice, and carried on staring at the blank screen in front of her.

"I'm glad you're not joining your friends tonight, Polly, they degrade you. They absolutely degrade you. They bring you down to that murky horrible gloom you were trapped in until you met me."

"I just want to escape," Polly nodded, hiding her repulsion as she sipped at the Martini again.

"But Charles, what's in it for you?"

She turned around to face him, laying her hand on top of the static palm that had melded itself into the skin of her thigh.

"I understand, I am to be at Hartlands. I can't wait. But for you to see me at Hartlands, will that be pleasure enough? Just to see me, and not to touch me?"

Polly spoke her words earnestly, without any hint of the red seduction of the lips she had painted last week at the Radisson.

"Think of me as a philanthropist, if you must think of me as anything at all. My intentions haven't changed since we met in that café back in Sussex. I meant what I said there, Polly, that beauty needs something to frame it, and I am giving that to you. Think of the age gap, thirty years and the rest. I don't need to be fooling around with you, Polly. I've had my fill of women, and of men too, for that matter. I think they diagnose it as world-weariness. It's not something you expected a man to say, is it Polly? That he doesn't want to sleep with you? Well I don't, and I thought you'd appreciate that. In your eyes I saw a woman above sex and the animalistic violence of the human bond. But you ask a good question. What is in it for me? I get to give you a gift, and let you live at Hartlands, living at Hartlands together. I can save you from the prosaic, and I don't need to touch you to do that."

He removed his hand from her thigh. Polly curved her lips into a slight smile, turning her body round to face him on the sofa.

"Thank you," she breathed, gently, holding his gaze and trying to diffuse it of all its threat.

"Go to bed now, you're tired," he replied, casting a fatherly look upon her.

She did as she was told, but she lay on top of the queen-sized bed with its unappetizing yellow colour, a disturbing shade of dehydrated urine. It was too hot to go beneath it, and the sweat was clammy on her bare skin. She lay in her white dressing gown, rigid along the top of the bed.

She let the sound of the traffic waft over her, all the laughing going on outside, and the clinking of the glasses that accompanied it. It must have been a Saturday; everybody on the streets sounded happy. There was a bar just down the road, and people must have been pouring out onto the streets with their chilled lagers and their flavoured ciders, all laughing and sweating and drinking away the weekend. They would probably go and lie in some park tomorrow and swelter, or retreat back into the countryside, hiding under the dappled shade of the comforting oak trees.

Polly could hear Charles moving about in the room next door. He was to sleep on the sofa. That was the arrangement. She might have been told, but she couldn't remember.

She thought of her mother in her little courtyard garden, so cold and fresh, it never got any of the sun. It was really so frustrating, the little nymph there, in the water fountain, but it was probably going to be subject to a hosepipe ban soon. She was under the same sun stripped sky though, certainly, and tomorrow Polly would be on a plane, flying away south, to Spain, for her honeymoon.

At least now she knew what to expect.

CHAPTER FOUR

Spain was a nightmare in heat and dust. But it wasn't the prospect of the unending rows of undulating mountains nor the lack of any shade that was the cause of Polly's newly acquired misery.

Charles did not really have a house in Spain, a big Spanish villa with a luxurious swimming pool. As she languished inside, in the bedroom of the poky little flat Charles called his own, Polly thought of the imaginary swimming pool and it mocked her in its bright blue luminescence.

Charles rented the apartment from wealthy expat friends, who had a farm and ran quirky retreats. Sometimes they hosted Buddhist monks, sometimes they hosted nudist colonies, but they mostly hosted artists, academics, writers, and Charles Carraway and his intelligence was one of their most vital and dependable resources.

They let him have the flat, free of charge, with its narrow kitchen, the living room in the centre that made Polly feel like she had been most decidedly locked away, and the double room that faced out towards the mountains. Looking out at the scorched terrain, with its stunted green trees, was the one benefit of her new situation. She could gaze far away, and pretend that she was traversing the track across the valley to the next village, sweating under the sweltering sun.

Charles had neglected to tell his friends that he had married again. They evidently knew his ex-wife, Pauline, and they spoke about her a lot. It seemed that they liked Pauline a bit more than they liked Polly, Polly who was not so warm and not so gregarious. She didn't drink, and that they could most certainly not understand, when it was a euro for a rosado, but she remained prim on her mineral water. They came to the unavoidable conclusion that she was pregnant, and that there would be another child at Hartlands soon. It had been so long since Alexander had last graced the nursery there, and it must be so strange now, the big old echoing house bereft of the sounds of youth and life.

The first night they arrived into a wall of heat. Charles decided that they should go to dinner, and eat tapas in Spain, there was nothing like it. Polly was not hungry. The flight had made her feel ill, as had the journey up the winding mountains, with Charles driving erratically around every twist and bend.

It had lapsed on to eight o'clock in the evening, and still they did not go to dinner.

Polly lay on the bed, dozing, whilst Charles read a book in the corner of the next room. She opened her eyes, stretching over with a great effort to check her watch, which she had left on the bedside table beside her. With her fingers that were still sleepy and sick she knocked it down and onto the cold tiled floor, and there it had broken, proclaiming the time to be nine thirty. She must have missed dinner, and she rolled over and closed her eyes, relieved that Charles had been kind enough not to wake her.

There was a knock at the door. It must be morning, Polly mused, as she opened her eyes and found herself wading through the sickly thrall of a migraine. But she discovered that it was still night, just past ten o'clock in the evening, and that they were about to go out to dinner.

"Do as the Spanish do!" Charles merrily chirped.

He had laughed to see her so wide eyed and pale upon the bed, distressed and confused at the new culture in which she found herself. She did not look so poised now.

"Come on Polly, my friends are waiting."

Polly, with some difficulty, got up from the bed and interrogated her reflection in the mirror. Her hair was up, and it could stay up, it looked neat, it looked perfectly acceptable. She wore long white trousers, and a black vest top. Both looked likewise to be perfectly acceptable for the late night tapas trip. But her face was clammy, and her mind was reeling against the stuffy heat and the need to go out and eat with these people she had never met before. But she resolved herself to it; and taking Charles' arm, she walked out of the flat, and into the restaurant.

On the scale of the most annoying women Polly had ever had the misfortune to encounter, if she had ever thought of recording such a tally, Gabriella Lefroy ranked highly, perhaps even topping the shortlist. Polly, sick and ill, had tried to tell Charles' friends that she had a migraine, but they would hear nothing of it. Instead, they chose a table next to a rousing flamenco band, and poured her a big glass of rosado. She was stuck with Gabriella, whilst Charles talked shop with her husband, Mike. Polly did not usually succumb to the mortal malaise of irritation; but Gabriella, as she munched upon her whole sardines, and stacked more croquetas onto Polly's plate, riled her very blood, as it fought against the rosado she had to sip at, and the dizzy unfamiliarity of her migraine.

"How young you look! Really, nothing more than a child. But we can still be best friends, can't we? I really shouldn't be saying this, but do you know how much you look like Pauline, Pauline Carraway? Charles' first wife? She was dark haired like you, only she had a bit more in the way of curves. She and Charles were such a handsome couple, and of course they had the most handsome of sons, Alexander. A little wild was Alexander, he nearly got himself expelled from Eton but thankfully Uncle Anthony stepped in and hushed it all up very nicely."

Polly didn't know who Uncle Anthony was, but then again she didn't really care that much. She was only half listening, the white shakes of sickness were rattling at the pit of her stomach, and whilst Gabriella remained stuck on her monologue she would not be called upon to talk.

"Of course, it was so sad when they divorced, fifteen years ago now, is it? And Pauline, going off with an Argentinean polo hand half her age to live with him on his father's cattle ranch. Well, I couldn't believe it either. I thought she'd be home in a month. Charles is charming, and so accommodating. Fancy, him marrying someone like you. What do you do exactly? Are you one of his students? Or do you write? We have a lot of authors around here, you know, you should be able to get some tips off them. It's never appealed to me myself, all that time alone staring at a blank screen."

Polly almost reeled with surprise when she realised that Gabriella had actually stopped for breath, and was interrogating her with keen, sharp little dark eyes.

"Actually, no, I don't write," Polly paused for a moment to clarify the meaning of her existence, "I, I shall be looking after Hartlands."

Gabriella drew a deep breath through her stout frame so the curls of her corkscrewed ginger hair wriggled and giggled like a myriad of deadly snakes.

"I shouldn't think Hartlands needs much looking after, myself. I believe the place runs like clockwork, like all these places do. But I suppose you're in it for the money. I have heard it's tough for young people like you to get a job in the economic climate we're in at the moment. I mean Mike and I find it hard enough getting people to come on our retreats. But yes, there must be so much competition for jobs, everybody's a graduate these days, and it must be so much easier just marrying Charles like this," Gabriella cooed patronisingly, her dark eyes gazing resolutely at Polly, "you are in it for the money, aren't you?"

"I'm sorry, I don't feel well."

Polly turned a pleading gaze at Charles, who was sat opposite her. But Charles didn't hear her mumbling protest against the wall of live music, and instead continued his academic conversation with his learned friend.

"I don't feel well," she reiterated, louder this time, as she placed her cutlery on the plate to reinforce the point.

"Pauline didn't get a penny when they divorced, you know. Well, she always was above those things, money didn't interest her, neither did Hartlands for that matter, and it turned out the polo hand's father was a big name, one of those top, top men you hear about in Argentina. He owned so many cattle ranches he didn't know what to do with them, and so she was quite set up as it turned out. But what will you do, tucked away in the country like that? You should think of running retreats. Mike resisted at first, but we haven't looked back, except for maybe the nudists. They have no shame, really, they don't."

Polly watched the clock above the bar intently until they finally got up and left for the night. Charles did not seem to mind as he watched her sighing across the table, her hands wobbling as she sipped her wine. He hadn't ordered her water like she had asked. He had instead suggested that the wine would help to sooth her stomach and make her feel better.

Indeed, Polly spent most of her time in Spain watching the clock. She would watch to see when Charles would be back from giving his lessons; he had efficiently planned his honeymoon to correspond with one of Gabriella and Mike's writing courses. She would watch the clock to see when he was due to return from one of the local bars. Mike was a big drinker. Charles never got drunk. Meanwhile Polly stayed in the little flat, claiming to be ill, which only reinforced Gabriella's conviction that she was pregnant.

And so it fell out, by the end of the fortnight, that Polly and Gabriella were not destined to become best friends. Instead it became Gabriella's habit, in every spare moment, to declare to her husband, and indeed to anyone else who happened to be in hearing, that Polly was proud, stuck up, vain, rude, and most despicably of all, definitely in it for the money rather than the art.

Polly's main feeling on leaving Spain was one of relief. And when she stepped into the cool air of Gatwick, now enjoying a lapse in the hot summer weather, which naturally follows news of a hosepipe ban, she felt like she had stepped outside of the club, and was ready to begin anew.

"I hope you don't keep a Mrs Danvers?" Polly mused, as she was driven up to Hartlands again.

Although it was a gloomy, overcast summer's day, the grass was freshly vibrant, a tonic to the brown swathes of dead vegetation that swamped the Spanish mountains.

"I told you Polly, it's just us."

She almost crossed her fingers in the hope that he was not going to recall the conversation at the Radisson. He hadn't referenced it for some days, which was a relief as it had grown tedious.

"A cleaner does come in once or twice a week. But that's all. It's just us, I promise."

This time, he did not lead her through the grand Victorian entrance on the west side of the house. They parked in the shadow of the north side, which was skirted by a high smooth wall, slightly overgrown with ivy, on the left. There was a little green door Polly had not noticed before, tucked away where the ivy-clad wall met with the house. It was certainly much less intimidating than the stuffy grandeur of the Victorian portico, and Polly smiled for the first time in two weeks.

She followed Charles inside. The green door led straight to a flight of stairs: up for the formal rooms, the drawing room, the dining room and suchlike, higher still there were the bedrooms, whilst it was down for the kitchen, and the snug little family rooms in which Charles had grown up.

"We don't generally use the upstairs rooms that much. The cleaner cleans them, and that's all really."

"Am I not to be their ornament?"

Polly smiled as they stepped down the cool, well-worn slabs of the stairs into the kitchen. Charles did not answer, and began to make some coffee, whilst Polly set about observing the room around her.

They were actually deep below the level of the ground, but the high ceilings and the length of the room created a sense of almost infinite, cavernous, space. Light fed in from the long narrow windows at the the top of the walls, along which ran a set of bars.

Polly felt trapped, and sat down at the long oak table, which Charles told her had been carved from a tree on the estate.

"There's not much of the estate left, as it happens. It's mostly been sold off, we've got some of the park, and the sheep, and the cemetery, but you wouldn't want to see that on your first proper day here, would you?"

Polly pulled her phone out of her pocket. She felt like she had better ring her mother, to tell her that she was safely home.

They had had an almighty falling out whilst she was in Spain, when she had rung to tell her the good news of her marriage. Polly did not have much to offer to the conversation, remaining silent and calm on the other line, far from her mother's pungent purple rage.

At first her mother's chief disgust was that she had not been invited to the wedding, as quiet an affair as it was. Then she had railed against the bitter and undeniable fact of Charles Carraway's age. She returned to loudly moaning about the lack of wedding invite, all the while sending scorching tears down the line so that Polly was almost pricked by their magnificent force. But still Polly remained quiet, which infuriated her mother all the more.

"You know, we don't get much in the way of signal here. It's somewhat of a black spot, down in the valley, it makes this strange kind of dipped effect. There's the landline, down in the snug, but the telephone's so old I doubt it works any more."

And so the Radisson dynamic continued: he crooned, he charmed, and above all, he controlled. Polly had been enchanted, before, by this glimpse of the other side of life, his conversation and antiquated manners carousing her beyond the mundanity of the world she knew too well. But he had begun to grate on her.

His every word was tainted by a faint smear of his upper-class masculinity, which reeked of port and cigar nights, velvet waistcoats and smoking jackets, runs in the first eleven and tries in the first fifteen, of an infinity spent in mansions and in castles, shooting pheasants and culling deer, raping and destroying servant wenches. Funny how he had not touched her since he had undone her wedding dress back in the Islington flat.

He now handed her a steaming cup of hot coffee, black, just as Polly liked it.

"I'm going to head into town now, just to pick up some food. You stay here, down here in the kitchen I mean. You can go into the snug if you like, and settle in. This is your home now, Polly, and I'm sure you'll learn to love it."

He might have leant down to kiss her cheek. But instead he picked up his keys from the oak table, and raced back up the cold flagstones, leaving his empty footsteps ringing round the room.

Polly slowly put her hands to her ears as if to block out the noise, and leant her elbows down on the table. She closed her eyes, and pictured the white Georgian drawing room in all its splendour. It was the thing that had brought her back here, to Hartlands, and it would set her free, surely, unlike this airy kitchen beneath the earth. So she got up from the table, bringing the coffee with her.

Polly soon found herself on the next level of the building, standing in front of a large white door. She had to exert some effort to push it open, and finally it creaked reluctantly open on its hinges, admitting her into the hall.

The hall was dingy and claustrophobic; all the doors around her were closed. Polly shivered, Charles was obviously not spending the fortune that was needed in order to heat the place, and she tried to remember which door was home to the white drawing room, her sanctuary.

She decided to try the first door on the left. It was locked. She tried the next door, and it too was locked. She began to shake the doorknob with furious frustration, the coffee swarming itself into a black tidal wave, nearly spilling out of the cup she held in her left hand. But it was no good, it would not open.

She took a sip of the coffee and tried the third door. It was locked. She tried the next, and Polly was so surprised to feel it give under the pressure of her hand that she nearly dropped her coffee cup.

The door swung open. Polly felt the suspense rise. She walked in, expecting another beautiful room, a red room, a green room, the room that would set her up as the jewel Charles had promised this house would make her.

But all she felt was dull anticlimax. The room was bare, completely bare, but for a ragged copy of *The Sun* that lay in the corner under a full mug of stagnant tea, the milk rising to the surface in awful despoiled magnificence.

Polly shivered again. The room was deathly cold, and disappointment gnawed at her bones. At least the view was lovely though; gazing out eastwards across the rolling lawns and tree-lined drive. With some bitterness, she hoped that she could count the lawns as part of the estate still.

She walked back into the hall, looking up, this time, to see the great old staircase winding its way up to the bedrooms. She had no inclination to go up there yet. She half-heartedly tried the three other doors: one of which was locked, and the other two swung open to reveal similar scenes of desolation.

Polly did not know what to do. She certainly did not want to return down into the kitchen. There she felt the weight of the earth crashing around her, folding her down into its loamy folds, an early grave, rotting beneath the dirt there where nobody would think to look. She thought of the snug. It sounded as though it might be less oppressive, so she returned back downstairs and into the basement.

The snug was aptly named, unlike the house it stood in. Whilst it had the high ceilings and the barred windows that could be found in the kitchen, it was thickly carpeted in warm claret magnificence. A heavy rug lounged in front of a large fireplace, the mantle littered by photographs of varying sizes and ages.

Polly sat down on the comfortable sofa, casting her eyes over the pictures, the assembled shadows and shades of Hartlands.

The photograph in the centre depicted a wedding. The bride looking back at her must have been Pauline. With her big black curly hair, she was an advert for the splendour of the late seventies. Her dress, however, was surprisingly delicate, and curiously like Polly's own. Pauline was a tall woman too, and the lace of her wedding dress clung to her, not like the baggy satin of the big pink white macaroon in which Polly's mother had been married.

Polly shuddered. She did not like to think of herself as Pauline's replacement. But the portrait of Pauline did not disturb her as much as the image of Charles, her groom, standing next to her. Charles, who had hardly changed in the intervening years, apart from his jet-black hair that had faded into a greyer shade of pale, looked so delightfully happy, like a young child surprised with the present of his dreams on Christmas Day. Polly attempted to smile back with him, instinctively removing her phone from her pocket as she did so.

She had asked one of the witnesses to take a photograph of her on her wedding day in Islington. She had not even thought to look at it before. She had put her phone away in her bag, and zipped it up tight. And so with Pauline's merry eyes on her, she looked at the photograph for the first time.

Polly did not look like herself in the picture, or even much like Pauline. She had a faraway look in her eyes, and a tight smile that looked through the camera. She had no substance, and was barely tangible, whilst Pauline, frozen by time, was still so very fleshy and vital. Charles she would not look at. She knew he would not look like the boyish man in the photograph on the mantlepiece, and nothing would ever bring that expression back into his world-weary eyes again. Weary of both men and women, surely that was impressive, she mused, as she drew her reluctant eyes over the other photographs.

The other photographs appeared to chart the childhood of Alexander Carraway, the son and heir to Hartlands, who must be pushing thirty now. Surrounded by big black Labradors, pictured on little sailing dinghies, and mounted on ponies that seemed to grow larger each time, Alexander looked like a lively child. They stopped when he was a certain age, about fifteen it seemed to Polly, of course, that must have been when he went away to Argentina with his mother.

Restless, Polly rose from the sofa and moved about the room again. Behind her, on a little table, stood a photo all on its own. It showed a young Charles Carraway, complete with dark hair and devastating tan, with a young and beautiful Latino woman on his arm. Polly understood. It was Alexander, older, and a married man in Argentina. It made her sad, staring at Alexander staring back at her without seeing anything.

A door banged upstairs. It was Charles, arrived back from town with the shopping. Polly stayed in the snug and waited for him to find her. But he did not come.

A jewel, a jewel for Hartlands. As she sat in the snug with its cosy carpet and nostalgic family memorabilia, his voice still found a way to mock her. What a bloody jewel in the crown she was now. She reflected that she should have just thrown her Martini all over him, the dirty bastard, preaching and lording it over her like that.

But Polly believed she could change it, that she could destroy the Radisson dynamic, which was deafened and defined by all his self-assurance and sleek grey-haired confidence. He would be defeated yet, once she had decided how it was to be done. She would bring him back down to the human level he despised, that she despised, but if she was to share Hartlands with him, they should at least be equals. He should not be so above her, a disembodied voice crooning all over her, so superior, ordering dirty Martinis, crushing her soul with all of his masterly proclamations.

They cooked dinner, or rather, Polly heated up the dinner prepared by the cleaning lady, whilst Charles put his feet up in the snug.

"She always does these meals for me," Charles said carelessly, as he explained about the duck in orange that lay under clingfilm in the fridge, "I thought you'd like to heat it up, Polly, get a feel of the AGA. I expect you haven't come across one before, have you?"

He lazed out across the sofa, resting his feet up on the small coffee table that was littered by expensive magazines: *Tatler*, *Vogue*, *Sussex Life*, all well past their sell-by dates, dusty and collecting dust as they lay beneath Charles' feet.

He opened some expensive-looking port, but didn't offer Polly any.

"There's some mineral water in the fridge, I thought you'd prefer it."

Polly nodded, and went to the fridge. She burned herself as she brought the duck in its royal blue baking tray out of the AGA, but Charles did not appear to notice. Sitting now at the oak table, he was engrossed by the port, and the newspaper by his side.

"As a rule I always think it's rude to read at dinner amongst company, but we're married now, Polly, aren't we? So it doesn't really count as company, does it?"

It had been a strained meal; Charles reading his newspaper, Polly picking at the duck. She disliked duck, immensely, and as a rule never generally ate it. But she was hungry, she had not eaten all day, and Charles had not provided her with lunch.

"Where's my bedroom?" Polly asked, as Charles continued to flick his eyes over *The Daily Telegraph*. "Where am I sleeping, Charles?"

"Where indeed?" Charles repeated, chuckling, drinking down the port in a big wolflike gulp. "I'm just playing, Polly, teasing you. You'll sleep down here, of course."

"Down here?"

Polly looked around, confounded, seeing only the kitchen and the snug and the door that led down to the little loo.

"Don't look so alarmed, Polly. There's a room off the snug, and that's where you'll sleep."

"Is it because the rooms upstairs are empty?" Polly demanded, finishing with the duck and gazing at him across the table.

"I told you not to go up there."

"I thought it was part of our deal, your philanthropy, the beautiful rooms for me to sit in?"

Polly sounded every syllable of the word phil-an-thropy, spitting it out like it was diseased, congealed vomit on her tongue.

"Many in your place would envy you, my dear."

"Why are some of the doors locked?"

"I'm not in the habit of repeating myself, Polly, but for your sake I'll make an exception just this once. I told you not to go up there, what don't you understand about that?"

Polly got up from the table, grazing the chair back on the cold flagstones. All she could do was to turn to the sink, where she began to run the water ready for washing up the plates, mounting her useless attempt at rebellion in this crushing act of domesticity.

"I'll guide you, protect you, but that might mean I have to tell you what to do, but you won't mind that, will you, Polly?"

His voice crashed away with the turbulence of the bubbles that swarmed in the hot water. She had squirted too much green liquid into the basin. But he was not talking, it was just that wretched conversation ringing in her ears again.

She scraped the mangled duck away into the bin and stopped the taps, plunging her hands into the scalding water. They turned red, red and vibrant and sore, but still she continued, rubbing the plates with angry frustration, scrubbing out the remnants of the duck and the orange and the conversation at the Radisson.

"There's tiramisu in the fridge," Charles offered, finally, when Polly had dried the plates and sat back down at the table.

She felt like storming off, but there was nowhere for her to go.

"I'm not hungry."

"So that's how you keep so slender," Charles laughed, pleased with his own feeble joke. "Do you want to see your room, then?"

"Where will you sleep?" Polly shot back.

"So you can seduce me in the middle of the night?"

"Don't be childish, Charles. I'm above those things, I don't know how to feel pleasure, remember?"

"I quite forgot, Polly, you cold, unfeeling, monster. I sleep upstairs. I don't think you'd be comfortable up there at the moment, as I'm yet to get your room renovated."

"Is it empty, like the other rooms?" she asked, a weariness creeping into her tone, as she idly passed her fingers around the rim of her glass.

"In a way. It's not ready for you, yet."

Charles folded up the newspaper and set it to the side.

"Will it look out across the valley?"

"It faces west."

West was out and down and across to the ridge and the fir trees that had chilled her with their singular sense of deadening claustrophobia. Polly would like to have screamed. And he might have read her thoughts, as he sat, looking at her across the table. But they were further apart than they had been at the Radisson; her, further away from him across the big oak table that could seat twelve easily.

"It's cool in the summer there," he added, impersonally.

"It'll be cold in the winter, too."

"Polly, why the impertinence? It's not like you."

He folded his arms, and then brought his right hand up to stroke his chin. He was weary, and he suddenly looked older in the dim light of the kitchen.

Charles liked to keep the kitchen dim. It reminded him of the days when Hartlands had no electricity, of the days when the kitchen would rarely be still apart from during the dead night.

Polly shook her head, almost yielding to him.

"I'm tired, Charles, tired and confused. But take me to bed, and I'll be fine."

Charles drew his eyebrows together, trying to read his new wife. Polly lazed with one elbow resting on the table, surveying the old oak with glassy eyes. Evidently, she did not mean that she wanted him, so he got up, and led her down into the snug, up a few steps in the corner of that room, through to where her bed lay. He shut the door on her, and smiling a quick smile of complete satisfaction, he returned to the kitchen to gulp down the tiramisu, demolishing Polly's portion too.

CHAPTER FIVE

Polly awoke to find soft sunlight creeping in at the high narrow window at the top of her new bedroom. She had completely forgotten where she was, and when she had woken up, the box-like anonymity of the room in which she had slept baffled her.

She raised herself gently up on the bed, the single bed, which was adorned by a charming little patchwork quilt embroidered in reds and yellows and blues. It was the only thing of warmth in the room. The only other item of furniture was a dusty chest of drawers that couched miserably in the corner, against which someone, presumably Charles, had placed her purple suitcase.

She shivered. Her head felt numb, her eyes swam with sleep, she was there, and not there, all at the same time.

Polly could not remember going to sleep. He had led her out of the kitchen with its dim lights and the warmth of the AGA, through the snug, which had grown cold, and into this room. She could not remember going to sleep, undressing, getting into bed.

She rolled onto her side, trying to identify·where she had left her phone. It was on the floor. As she did so, she realised that she was still wearing her jeans, and a little maroon vest top. The wire of the bra dug into her back; it was that lacy white one from the wedding.

The prick of the bra jolted her memory. She had been so tired by it all, arriving at Hartlands as the new lady of the manor, that she had collapsed into bed without even bothering to remove her clothes, and put on her pyjamas, which were still packed away in her unopened suitcase.

As she picked up her phone and slid the lock key down, her eyes were stung by the unnatural brightness of the screen. The digits of the time stood out, dancing and lurid. Polly chuckled. It was eight o'clock in the morning, and she always woke up at eight o'clock in the morning, whether she and her friends had been out or not, whether she had had only five hours' sleep, or two, as happened some nights. Polly was unashamedly a creature of habit, and she smiled. Even Hartlands with its dusty pall, its lurking shades, its high ceilings and its locked rooms, had not destroyed the strength of her habit.

But perhaps it had destroyed her purpose. She sat on the edge of the bed, wondering what she must do today. She felt bereft, she had no timetables or schedules or lists written in a neat hand and enlivened by bright colours and a splash of glitter. All Polly had was the house, crouched in its slumbering sublimity, fading intolerably back into the earth.

The house would not tell her what to do like Charles had promised it would. She must construct it for herself, and to that end Polly decided that she would explore every inch of the dwindling estate outside, the cemetery, the sheep, the lawns. Upstairs and downstairs, she would build Hartlands afresh in her mind.

It would be hers, and she would begin today, and she would call her mother and try to reason with her. But this drag of the mundane frightened and appalled her; she wanted to be left to commune with the house, and this was her perk of the deal, surely, the deal they had bartered together at the Radisson that mild night in June?

"You'll have Hartlands all to yourself, Polly, but you won't mind that, will you?"

She heard Charles' words, but he was not there when she walked into the kitchen. She wondered where he might be, so early on a Sunday morning. Church? She smiled weakly at the notion, thinking vaguely of the nearest village and its statement church tower.

Her mother had once been in raptures about that tower, and had dragged her to a fundraising auction in its honour at the village hall. They hadn't bought anything, of course, all the lots were far too expensive, but it was a pleasure to gawp at everybody else with their ready money to spend in that noble purpose of saving the beautiful tower. But they had been trying to save the tower for the last ten years, and her mother had begun to suspect that the parish had quite enough money now to keep it standing for at least another century or two.

Polly sat down at the kitchen table, and tried to plan her day. She had to somehow escape from the haze of her new life as Mrs Polly Carraway, the mistress of Hartlands. It was like she had not been present in the last two, three, four, weeks. It was all a blur, an experience only for the lady in the mirror who had looked like a fairy-tale princess, who had walked into the town hall in Islington, and who had stepped on a plane to fly far away. But here she was, and this was what she had wanted, she had told Charles, down the telephone, at her graduation and of course, fatefully, at the Radisson, that she wanted Hartlands. And here it was, around her, on top of her, shoving her rudely down into the ground beneath it.

Polly smiled, a secret type of smile. She wanted to see where Charles was. So she scraped back the chair and walked up the steps into the main belly of the house, calling out his name. But stasis answered as it had the day before, as she plunged back into the hall, the curtains and blinds all pulled down around her.

Her voice echoed uncannily about the place, reverberating out of unseen corners, traversing into little pockets of space she could not see, and would never see. Surely she could not see all of Hartlands in a lifetime.

She tried opening all the doors again with the same result: some were locked, and the others were empty. With all this banging around, the hallooing that had begun to hurt her throat, she thought that Charles would surely have heard her and come down the stairs to chide her presumption in exploring a house that was now her own.

Polly walked into one of the empty rooms. It faced north, to where they had parked the Aston Martin yesterday. Her feet, clad only in thin socks, were chilled by the frosty oak floor beneath. The room around her seemed to breathe out big damp gulps of air. Indeed, the staleness seeped out of the sickly wallpaper, which hung from the walls like the folds of a woman's skirt as she stood, laughing, half-undressed, frozen in teasing and tantalising paralysis.

Polly walked over to one of the windows, avoiding the nails that were scattered about on the floor, which rattled away along the floorboards as she stepped near them, as if she was participating in some childish game. Eventually, she reached the window, and saw that Charles' car was not there. But she had expected that.

She turned back to face the room, which ached in its desolation and its need for careful restoration. Polly ran her fingers lightly across the wallpaper, her soothing touch almost blessing the walls.

Once, surely, it must have been grand. In this morgue of faded Palladian splendour, she thought of the white room, and was impatient to see it again.

"Do you like it then?"

Charles was watching her face, and all its subtle flickers of expression, as she took in the white walls of the room around them, the chairs and long sofa upholstered in the same pure colour, the original Georgian relics that they were. The bare oak floor, and the large mirror with gilt edgings, which reflected the view of the valley beyond so it was impossible to determine where the outside began, gave the room a light, airy, and timelessly sophisticated feel.

"You seemed so desperate to see it, I had no choice but to open up the doors again."

"It's far more beautiful than I could have ever expected. If I were you I wouldn't be able to stay away."

"You dressed for the room," Charles said, when he first saw Polly in her wedding dress at Islington town hall, "minutely."

Polly knew that what she was wearing was not what she would usually wear at all. She should be wearing bright white, plain, completely unblemished, only by its striking tailored lines. There would be no salute to sentiment in lacy seams and sequins. It would be pure Polly, her head high and her soul cold and proud. But she knew that when she was drawn to that dress she was thinking of herself at Hartlands. In this dingy, damp, room she wanted to put the dress back on, and help restore it to its finery.

Distracted, she let her head fall against the walls of the big beautiful house, as if she expected to collapse into its embrace, the house to rally round her and warm her frosted body. Although she did not feel the power of the house's majesty flooding into her veins, she felt some sense of camaraderie oozing from its barrenness. She pressed down one of the huge hanging folds of wallpaper, as if she could restore it to the walls, and returned back down into the kitchen.

Polly, having changed into fresh clothes, stepped out of the green door at the back of the house, to emerge into shade, the continuation of that dark gloom that eddied throughout Hartlands. Crunching the gravel of the drive under her feet, she began to walk around the house, past the ridge with its yawning shadows, until she turned the corner round into the sunlight. It was a warm and rather pleasant day for the end of July. There was the odd cloud scattered about, but the sky was mostly blue.

Polly let the warm rays tingle over her cold body. She smiled as she stood in reverent appreciation, feeling the respectful English sun shine over her pale skin. The sun's glowing rays revivified her to a certain extent; they did not extinguish her as they had done in Spain. Here she could breathe, and she remained still, looking down the valley before her. As she looked, it was as if she saw Charles and herself, an innocent spectre of months past, leaning on the stile over in the little copse she saw nestled, half a mile away.

He had led her through the little copse, where the trees were bare and a few daffodils lay blithely beneath the spindly branches of the silver birches. Polly was angry. He had promised her the prospect of his house, Hartlands, but here they were instead ambling through the dreary spring countryside with not a stately home in sight.

But her anger subsided, evaporating almost completely, when the copse stopped abruptly and folded out into a series of wide green rolling fields. At the end of the crevasse of green lay Hartlands.

The house must have been sat about half a mile away, at the end of a sweeping valley that was dotted here and there with sheep.

But the sheep did not concern Polly, who was struck by the peculiar notion that the house should be rising from its slumbers to take her by the hand and offer her a greeting. And yet, the house was not so solicitous. It stubbornly looked away from her, its front elevation facing into a steep ridge of trees off towards the west. She could not understand it, this house, which chose not to interrogate the sweeping views of the glorious South Downs, but instead to embroil itself within the darkness of the distant pines.

And Polly had forgotten Charles, who stood beside her still. She felt like she could forget him forever, if she could just belong to this house. She had finally found what she had been missing for all of her life, and it was not of flesh and blood, but built firmly out of bricks and mortar.

Charles had been right about one thing, though. Hartlands had been waiting for something, and Polly now felt sure that it had been waiting for her.

"In case you're wondering Polly, the ancestors named it Hartlands because one could always find harts, you know, male deer, congregating about the place. But the history of the spot is something else altogether. The family legend has it that my forebears were out hunting when they saw a beautiful woman, dressed all in white, flitting through the forest. Instead of pursuing their quarry, they pursued her, but rather than this ethereal creature being some spectral fancy like the hunters supposed, she was something decidedly more mortal, made out of flesh like the rest of us. They raped her, just there, on the hillside, or so they say."

The sun had made Polly forget why she was standing there in the great calm surrounds of the countryside, swathed and nurtured by the green fields around her, the sky that was heaped with gentle clouds, spreading out and down to the horizon. She was not looking back; looking back meant confronting the house and its extraordinary stifling gloom.

She was now stood on the south side of Hartlands, on a stretch of paving that lasted for a couple of yards, before it fell down a slope of rough green grass leading to the meadows of the valley, fit only for grazing sheep. But Polly had no inclination to tumble down the slope, nor to run across the valley to meet with the girl she had once been. So she turned back to face the house once more.

Immediately her attention was caught by the windows. Heavy shutters were drawn across them from the inside. Everything seemed denied to her.

Slowly, she walked across to the window she suspected hid the white drawing room from her, and turning her back on it with impatient frustration, she stood staring down the valley for the second time that day. But she would not give up, she was determined to explore this house and have what was hers, so she returned to the window, desperately trying to find some chink or crevice that would show her that vision of reassuring Georgian calm.

The frustration and the heat of the July sun burnt at her cheeks. She did not feel it, however, as she pushed her body closer to the window, her breath cloudy against the grimy glass. She pressed herself closer, and closer again, trying to merge herself to the memories of the room beyond. Pretty, pretty, Polly, in her perfect white splendour, he had said something like that. But now she could not remember, as she moved her hands to the window frame with its white peeling paint, pushing the glass in front of her upwards and stepping away, surprised that it had given so easily under her touch.

Polly was now breaking into her own home. She paused, in case a burglar alarm sounded. But the house was as quiet, and as still as before.

She lifted up the window fully so that she could actually climb into the room. She looked around, and felt desperately like she was in some child's adventure story, an Enid Blyton epic, and any second later she would be sat around drinking ginger beer and eating tongue. The sound of tongue appalled her, even more than the notion of duck in orange.

She pushed at the shutters, and they folded back to reveal her Georgian white drawing room, perfect, shining in the sun. Polly climbed through the window, and sat down in that room where she belonged.

A couple of hours must have pushed past while Polly sat there, contemplating, as the sunlight crept through the glass and slid down her cold cheeks. The room recharged her, and reminded her why she was there at Hartlands. After all, she had sacrificed everything for this quiet noble splendour that was all hers, or at least mostly hers. There was that problem with Charles. She knew he'd come back, eventually, and be infuriating. She pondered how she could drag him away from that constant flow of polished conversation she had thought that she would love. His words now only served to cast a shadow over her vital connection with the house and the escape it offered to her so very generously. She wondered how she could defeat him, but the sunlight lulled her bitter thoughts, and made her think that he could be defeated some other day.

Much as Polly would have liked to have stayed in a state of stupor, lolling on the delicate white sofa in its white drawing room, she knew that she had to call her mother. She was not sure what she was going to say to her, however. Maybe she could invite her over for tea, in the kitchen, and then show her the white room. Polly was not sure whether her mother would appreciate seeing the room, or the fact that she would have to clamber through a window in order to see it, but she guessed that by now, after a month's absence and a lifetime of emotions, her mother would probably want to see her younger daughter.

After trying the door, which remained locked and lacked the benefit of a key, Polly climbed back out of the window. But she could not bear for the room to be completely shuttered off from the world, dimmed and hidden behind heavy planks of wood. So when she drew the shutters together, she left a little gap, just so a little glimmer of light could illuminate the room still.

Now she had to set about finding some signal for her phone. Although the ridge shrouding the west side of the house repelled her, it was the highest edge of the valley, and so the most likely place where she could find signal. After deliberating for some time about how best she could reach the top, Polly located a rough path that looked as though it might carry her there. So she followed it as it wound up the perilous slope, the thick bracken impeding her progress several times. But eventually she climbed the summit, and there, mingling amongst the fir trees, she achieved her goal. Polly had signal at last.

She dialled the number and waited. Her mother eventually answered. Polly could plainly hear all of the pain and confusion in her voice. For once, Moira did not know what to say. It was, however, only a temporary lapse, as she continued to berate her like she had done when Polly had delivered her the happy news regarding her marriage.

"I've been worried sick about you! I've been absolutely beside myself, worrying about whether the plane had gone down, or whether you had been in a car crash. How am I supposed to know if something happens to you?"

Polly tried to speak, but was unsuccessful in her attempt, as her mother had not paused to let her have her right of reply.

"You have driven me mad, but thank goodness your sister and her new boyfriend are coming to visit me later this afternoon. She has been so good to me, your poor old mother, and when I think about how you've treated me, running off with that old man, it's diabolical. Other mothers would have disowned you. That's right, Polly, disowned you."

"I thought you might like to come up and visit," Polly mumbled, feeling the chill of the fir trees around her, her toes laced on the edge of the ridge, so careless about their perilous position between life and death.

"I won't meet that man," Moira replied, sharply, "I will not meet him."

"You won't have to," Polly explained, "you see, Mum, I'm alone here at the moment."

Her mother went silent. Polly drew the phone away from her ear to see if she had lost the connection, but the call was still live, and two bars of signal weakly flashed as if to prove it.

"Alone?" her mother repeated, the shock ringing in her voice. "He left you alone in that big old house? No bodyguard? Burglar alarm? Dog? Panic button? So he just leaves you there for the murderers and thieves and the drugged crazed squatters to come and rape you and murder you! And the youths who come up and drink at these places and get high, what will they do when they find you? With nobody to hear you scream? And then the gypsies, they might just turn up too, I've heard they've got a huge list of abandoned houses and they just pick one, like that, they'll make you their slave or something. Alone! I can't believe how irresponsible that man is. He ought to be struck off."

Polly had no reply for this. Tentatively, she repeated her earlier invitation for her mother to come and visit her that afternoon. But her mother was resolute, she would not come, and besides, she was looking forward to the visit of Polly's elder sister Petunia, and her new boyfriend, Jeremy.

Polly sighed, hung up, and kicked the loose earth around her. And then, with some difficulty, she descended the rough path, bending over every now and then to separate the fronds of bracken, so she did not trip over them down into oblivion. She went back into her bedroom, sitting down heavily on the patchwork quilt of her bed, and waited for the night.

It got darker as the day sashayed merrily into night, oblivious of Polly and her growing festering fears. Her mother's words had scorched her, and taught her to be afraid. She had dismissed them as ridiculous at the time; youths armed with flick knives and professional burglars equipped with silenced revolvers, the product of an overnourished imagination fed on reruns of *Midsomer Murders*, but now her fears had grown stronger than her reason.

She sat in the kitchen, grasping onto the daylight as a kind of hope, as a kind of salvation, that she would be safe. She tried to remind herself that her mother's words were, after all, those of a hysterical middle-aged lady with too much time on her hands and the propensity to actually believe what was written in *The Daily Mail*.

Charles still had not returned. Polly looked in the fridge, only to find more duck in orange, and shuddered. There was nothing else: some milk, a bit of brie and a packet of foie gras. And the rest of the world starves, Polly thought scornfully, going to the tap and pouring herself some water.

She had not eaten all day, and there was nothing to tempt her in the fridge. She wondered again where Charles might be. She felt cold, the AGA did not seem to be working, and she was not middle class enough to know how to go about fixing it. She had tried to lock the green outside door, but she could not find a key for it, and as a result she felt unusually jumpy, alone in this big old house she wanted all to herself.

She went to the snug, deciding that she might try to numb her fears by switching on the television. The television was a relatively ancient thing now; it was at least fifteen years old and a bit of a box. She tried to switch it on. All she got was the angry fizzle of white noise. It burred wildly until it collapsed into an empty black screen, which shook slightly, blinking into life every now and then. Polly smiled ruefully. At least Charles could not flick through the channels when she was trying to talk to him.

Beside the television there was a pile of old-fashioned videos. When Polly plugged in the VHS player its light flicked on encouragingly, but then it gave a great howl, an electric fizz, and died, died there in her arms.

Her phone battery was also beginning to run down. She abandoned it in her room. There was nothing else to do, so she slipped her hands down to the coffee table, and picked up the September 1999 edition of *Vogue* magazine. A fierce model stared back at her, as she plunged into its dusty recesses, curled up on the chair in the snug, the television broken, the video player broken, no sight nor sound of anything remotely technological, just Gisele Bundchen with her legs splayed open at an alarming angle, her face mannish, her gaze intense.

She fell asleep like that, *Vogue* on her lap, the September 1999 edition. Charles came back just before midnight and smiled vaguely to see Polly so undefended, sleep freezing her at a perfect moment of innocence and calm. She was in so deep a sleep that it did not look like she was dreaming; she was so still, so charming, so like a child.

Charles bent down over her, and listened to her low and steady breaths. He must have made some movement though, as her eyelids flicked open to reveal him standing, couched, like a predator, over her still and sleeping body.

"Go back to sleep," he said, with a hint of paternal affection in the command, "there, go back to sleep."

Polly shook her head, and with a great effort she was awake again. She sat up, and stared at him.

"What time is it?"

"There's a clock in the kitchen," Charles replied, standing up to pace the small rug.

"It's stuck. It says it's eleven, always."

"A place like Hartlands is timeless, though, is it not?"

"I wish you'd stop talking like that time at the Radisson."

"Are you drunk?" Any affection had slid out of his tone, and he now regarded her with flicking, gleaming, eyes. "Have you been drinking the port?"

"I don't drink, at least, I don't any more."

"Good."

He turned, about to go back into the kitchen.

"Where do you sleep?" she asked, again, half to herself, half to the air around her, the little room of the snug with its rows and rows of photographs all staring back at her, watching her, judging her movements with the same fixed expressions of temporary happiness. "Where do you sleep?"

"Does it matter, Polly?" Charles asked, having caught her floating words like a hunter, his ancestors, his father, his grandfather, riding across the estate hating and hallooing, the wildlife disappearing from their path, the guns cocked, the dogs primed, the horses heaving and hurling them over the hedges, and there was Charles with his captive deer, curled up on a chair in the snug, demanding to know where he closed his eyes and forgot it all. "Polly, I wish you'd stop asking all these questions. Is it not good enough for you that you're at Hartlands now?"

"You left me alone all day. But it was going to be you and I, you promised that."

"I say a lot of things," he returned, glass in hand.

He had reverted to the whisky, all over again.

"I'm afraid," Polly's voice quivered, her reserve vanished.

She thought of the lonely hours spent surviving dusk in the kitchen, trying to ignore the palpable sounds around her. It's an old house, it creaks. They might sound like footsteps, but they're actually not, they're mice, wandering around up there. There's a tap running somewhere, but it's really just the pipes, yes, that's it, it's the pipes moaning and humming.

It would be better, when they came, for them to just knock you round the back of the head, so you didn't know that they were even there, so you didn't know what had quite literally hit you. Then you wouldn't attempt to hide somewhere, watching them come in and seeing what weapons they had with them. Then you would know how they were going to hurt you, whether or not they were going to slice you open or send a bullet through your brains.

It's an old house, it will creak and moan. It sounded like something Charles had said, but it was her mother's words that had turned Hartlands from a paradise into a hell of dirty mortal fears.

"Afraid? Of me?" He chuckled, but not with mirth. "Polly, you're sensible enough to know that it's an old house, and it's certainly not haunted."

If Polly had been the raped woman in the white dress, she certainly would have hung around Hartlands making its inhabitants' lives as unpleasant as possible. She had probably ran mad, ostracised, pregnant with a child that nobody could claim, multiple fathers, all against her will. She had every right to haunt the place. And Polly was not afraid of her.

"Is this another game, Charles? You do so love to be cryptic. I thought it was all enigmatic conversation, trial by intellect, and we won't touch one another, I know, we won't do that, but can't we live together as civilised human beings, at the very least?"

Polly was tired, dazed, and so she laboured over the words she had been conjuring over and over again to herself. But he wasn't even there, he was striding about the kitchen, she could hear the soles of his shoes pounding themselves against the cold flagstones in a regular, rhythmic beat.

And so ended that day, Polly asleep on the sofa, waking up shivering in the night that was so very dark, with no blanket wrapped thoughtfully around her. So she crawled up into her little bedroom, the one that was so like a cell, and slept another couple of hours of blank black dreams.

CHAPTER SIX

Polly woke up at her regular time, as was her habit. But she could not know it, because her phone had died during the night, and as her watch had broken and the clock had stopped in the kitchen, she had no other way of telling the time.

"Time," she remembered him telling her, perhaps down the phone, she could not recall, "you don't need time at Hartlands, it's so very refreshing."

Polly pulled herself out of her sleepy paralysis. She must charge her phone, and climb back out onto the ridge to try and reason with her mother, and perhaps text some of her friends from university. She had forgotten to do that yesterday.

Polly being Polly had a special place where she kept her charger, in a secret little pocket of her suitcase. But when she slipped out of bed and opened the case, she found it wasn't there. Perhaps it was in an unthinkable moment of madness in the Spanish heat that she had overturned any hint of her obsessive compulsiveness and had stuffed the charger elsewhere. So she rifled through the rest of the case, her clothes, her toiletries and the condoms she had bought when she was uncertain as to whether Charles wanted to touch her or not. But it was not there. She ran into the kitchen, intent on confronting her new husband.

There was an unfamiliar female figure standing by the sink, whilst Charles was nowhere to be seen. Polly glided into the room, and sat down. The figure jumped as she heard the chair move, and swung round, all washing-up gloves and apron strings and bubbles from the sink.

"Good lord, you made me jump, Pauline!"

Polly narrowed her eyes and looked at her cynically, her gaze diluted with an ounce of pity.

"It's Polly, and I don't believe we've met."

"Polly, of course, it is quite similar to Pauline, and you are too, for that matter. I'm Nelly Harrison, by the way. I keep the house."

So Nelly Harrison kept the house, then. Polly was silent. She was going to keep the house, and the house was going to keep her. It was all part of the deal.

"Have you seen Charles this morning?" Polly asked, after a prolonged silence.

She wanted to snap at her, this apparition at the sink, with her loud flowered apron and short curly hair, frizzled to a greying brown. She did not seem part of Hartlands, standing there, washing up what Polly knew not, probably more duck in orange, she thought bitterly.

"Yes, dear, so I have."

Nelly Harrison's voice might have been a vintage preserved from the old days in Sussex. It was difficult now to find any quaint relic of a rural past that had been all but demolished in a county plagued by Londoners with their second homes, and the old in their retirement homes down beside the sea. Yes, Nelly Harrison may well have had an original Sussex accent. She might have buttered her wig, and beat the Devil round the gooseberry bush, all the while clinging onto the remnants of a strong pagan past. Sussex, according to the ever Venerable Bede, was the penultimate county in England to be Christianised. And so Nelly Harrison may well have spied witches in the woods, have partaken in cat burnings during the deep night, and walked through orchards haunted by dancing oranges.

Polly, whose parents had come down from London, had once laughed at the bizarre history of her adopted home. But she was not laughing now, not with Nelly Harrison standing in front of her, the daughter, the granddaughter, the great-granddaughter of the county that wunt be druv. Good lord no, Nelly Harrison was giving nothing away.

"Is he still here?" Polly asked, frustrated.

"No dear, Mr Carraway's gone to town."

Perhaps if Polly had indeed been Pauline Nelly Harrison may well have been a little more talkative. As it was, she carried on with her washing up. She plunged a saucepan into the bubbles; perhaps Charles had consumed a fried breakfast before heading off to Petworth, which would certainly account for the waft of bacon that still hung tangibly in the room. Also amongst the foam, Polly, with some horror, thought she could discern one of the containers that the duck in orange was usually cooked in.

"When's he going to be back?"

"He usually stays in Lunnon for the weekdays, and comes back home on the weekends."

It was then that Polly realised her mistake. Town meant the little town down the road to her, where there was a supermarket and some groaning antique shops, not the place that lay fifty miles away, where the cars rattled and the nights were infernos. Nelly Harrison meant London, and Charles had left her here, with his housekeeper, who would hardly talk, and stacks, and stacks, of her duck in orange.

"Has he left me any food?" Polly asked, the image of all the ducks that would have to die in order to fill her fridge swimming across her mind in a comical procession set to jumping jovial cartoon music.

"I see to that," Nelly Harrison said, as she turned from the sink, and opened a cupboard to reveal a mop, a broom, and a red bucket of assorted cleaning products. "Now, if you don't mind, I can't be chatting. I've got a house to clean."

She walked away, up the steps, and left Polly alone in the kitchen, idly strumming her fingers on the oak table.

Polly then got up, got dressed, and wondered what she should do, what she was meant to do. She felt herself becoming unable to plan her day. There was nothing, really, for her to do, and he had said that it would be like that. But she thought then that a life of idleness meant at least something to do: books to read, and to file away in the library, plates to polish, the silver to bring up to a stunning shine, maybe even liaising with the estate manager, which fields to plough, which sheep to sell. Instead, she stood in the kitchen, the soft summer light creeping in through the narrow, high windows.

She looked around her, and began to climb the stairs. This time she climbed them to the first floor, where she supposed he slept. It was the only logical explanation, and she would burn him with her logic yet.

Upstairs was coolly polished. She nearly slid on the smooth floorboards as she opened the heavy baize door that led out onto the landing, which hung, suspended, as it slunk towards the simply carved oak balustrade, and the winding square staircase that led back down into the house. There were no ornaments up here; it was plain, and chill, save for a few cheap-looking rugs that were strewn over the empty floor.

None of the doors that were littered about the landing were open. Polly sighed. She was bored of the extended game of hide and seek that the house and Charles seemed to be so expertly playing with her. Nevertheless, she stepped towards the first door, the door she was drawn to because she supposed it was the one that was going to be hers, and soon she would be living there, looking out west to the ridge of oppressive fir trees, and the monkey puzzles that were intermingled with them.

"Some of the ancestors obviously had a sense of humour," Charles had laughed, "those monkey puzzle trees are bizarre, deliciously bizarre."

The doorknob gave immediately under her touch. The door had evidently been recently oiled, and it swung smoothly open on its hinges. Polly walked in, surveying the room with her level gaze. It was a boy's room: some football posters on the walls, a Manchester United strip on the bed, action men and dinosaurs lying on top of one another in deep plastic boxes, static and waiting for their owner to return.

Polly sat down on the bed, unaware of the monkey puzzles and the firs that lurked like grim spectres outside the window, watching her with steady, unwavering suspicion. There was no breeze.

She could guess enough to feel that this was Alexander Carraway's room, the boy who had been taken by his mother to Argentina. This room Charles had evidently kept as a shrine, she supposed, or just in case Alexander returned. He would not care for it now he was a man, as this room belonged to a boy, with its action men and dusty dinosaurs lying forsaken, hoping to be played with again.

Perhaps Charles did feel, at the end of it all. And perhaps he was mourning, and not quite ready for Polly to be in this room at Hartlands yet. But Alexander would not return here, from the heat of Argentina with his glamorous young wife. He might even have children of his own, now.

Polly pitched forward off from the bed and wrangled with the boxes of action men to pick up one of the dinosaurs. She rubbed it free from its greasy layer of congealed dust, watching as the little flaky particles hit the light and meandered lazily around the room. She could clean these old toys up, then.

Polly had begun to lay out the dinosaurs and the action men on the rug, when the door banged open and Nelly Harrison stood in the room, dusters and polish waving in her hands. Polly raised her head to gaze coolly back at her. There was nothing but disdain in her stare, and Nelly Harrison felt the icy chill like someone had walked over her grave.

"I'm sure Mr Carraway would want this room left."

"But these toys are in a sorry state," Polly replied, evenly, rubbing her finger down the back of another mucky green dinosaur to reveal a perfect strip of bright, vibrant, colour.

"No one will be playing with them anytime soon. It's a funny enough thing to find you here, on your hands and knees with the old toys. I'd leave them alone, if I were you. Besides, Mr Carraway didn't want you up here, anyway."

Polly swivelled up from her position on the floor, the toys in ordered rows about her ankles.

"It's my house too, you know," Polly said, as if to convince herself, and not Nelly Harrison, standing with the polish and dusters, witnesses to her shame, her audacity in exploring a house that was hers, hers since the wedding in Islington and the issuing of the certificate that Charles had neatly stowed away in his briefcase.

Nelly Harrison cocked her head at her, slowly rotating it like a queasy, gormless owl.

"Hartlands don't belong to no one, it never has."

Polly smiled at her, and almost wanted to laugh. Like a hysteric, the rising mirth in her heart was bitter and cruel and just.

"I'll see the rest of these rooms," she affirmed, passing Nelly Harrison in the doorway with her dusters and her polish, "if you don't mind, of course, and then I'll disappear."

With a bitter kick fluttering at her usually stony heart, Polly felt the irony of the lady of the house having to beg to see its rooms. She moved down the corridor, and found a bathroom in the next room. It was a damn sight more appealing than the shoddy shower downstairs that piped out fizzling little spurts of hot water, scalding Polly's skin bright red, only then to lapse into frigid, frightened drops of ice, which dolloped down onto the green mould beneath her feet.

Nelly Harrison followed her all the time, like a bodyguard. Polly passed into the next room, a room she would have actually begged for, as it faced out across the green folds of the valley. In its delicate spaciousness it was so cruelly unlike her room downstairs, which kept her boxed up in a coffin of great airy dampness.

She could sense Charles in this room; it was most certainly his. There were a plethora of books scattered about, mostly his own titles, and other obscure bits of academe, those scholarly journals through which apathetic students scour desperately the night before their exams.

Polly was drawn to a lovely mahogany wardrobe, which was filled to the brim with Charles' crisp suits, his shirts, and beneath that, in the drawers, were his trousers, all perfectly pressed. All the while the valley outside shone rich and green and verdant. It was a marvellous room, and the folds of his bed were white, white and made fresh by Fairy and Nelly Harrison, who hovered like an omen behind her, her face crooked and sharp.

It was a room Polly could have loved, did love, and as she paused by the window she felt like Elizabeth Bennet surveying Pemberley for the first time. She could have been mistress of all this, and it was why she married Darcy, after all, so that she could walk in the magnificent shrubberies of Pemberley. Yet I am its mistress, Polly pondered, pausing still, lost somewhere between ownership and inadequacy.

Nelly Harrison continued to dust around her, rubbing down the great mahogany wardrobe, straining on her tiptoes to root out more dirt and destruction with her little feather duster. Polly passed her, her ordered thoughts lapsing into a confused mess, her face unreadable as ever, cold and given expression only by her taught cheekbones.

Nelly Harrison knew what Polly would try to do next. It was only logical, surely, the next room down the corridor, waiting there for her to step into. She was dusting one of the bedside tables, strewn with Charles' debris – a wine glass, *Daniel Deronda*, and some sleeping tablets – when she heard Polly wrestling with the doorknob out on the landing, her quiet whispered oath beating its flight out and down into the hall, and finally into the ears of Nelly Harrison, who knew that it would come.

She stepped back out onto the landing, and found Polly as she expected to find her, the child in the fairy story who would try every door before she was truly satisfied.

"I would not bother," Nelly Harrison said, enunciating the words clearly as if Polly was truly a child. But there was nothing childish about Polly, with her dark hair, her black hair, which was so cruel against her pale skin. "That room was Pauline's, and is never opened."

Polly turned her eyes back onto Nelly Harrison. Nelly Harrison thought they glistened with tears, as they were so dilated, an unnatural blue, so very different from the light bright ice of Charles Carraway's eyes.

Nelly Harrison braced herself for a fight. She truly never dusted Pauline's room, even though she had liked Pauline. She had been so chatty and sociable, flitting about the place, riding ponies and driving fast cars, always with a smile, a big smile, with those big lips that consumed most of her face. She would lean her head back and swallow you whole with that smile.

Pauline would always stop and chat, and be interested to hear about Nelly Harrison's second cousin on her mother's side, her with the cats, and Great Aunt Iris, and her pneumonia. Pauline would ask her to do dinner parties, and open up the dining room downstairs, and people from London would come down, exotic people, smoking cigarettes and other stuff besides.

She did not clean that room, though, since they knew what Pauline had done, with her big bouffant hair, which she had tamed into a sleek Diana bob by the nineties. It had not suited her. But she did not clean the room. It was as it was, and nobody need see it now.

"I understand," Polly said to Nelly Harrison, in a quiet voice, and Nelly Harrison's thin lips quivered as if insulted.

She had girded herself for this argument, this debate, the conjuring of the memory of Pauline Carraway owning Hartlands in the way that only Pauline could. But she had never really cared about Hartlands, after all, that was the problem, and Argentina was so far away. No, Pauline could not have cared.

Nelly Harrison watched as Polly turned back onto the landing. She did not descend the sweeping staircase like Pauline would have done in one of her fine Gucci frocks, but instead she retreated to the door that was formerly only ever used by the servants. Once, Hartlands would have been swarming with them, seeing to the icehouse, feeding the hounds, stirring the food and fuelling the fires, a big old machine worked by Nelly Harrison's ancestors.

Now Nelly Harrison could not help but watch as Polly, so graceful, so staid and polished, yet without that vim and violent vitality of Pauline, swept across in front of her. Polly then reached the big heavy door, pushed it open, and disappeared back down the stairs.

Nelly Harrison paused for a second, the duster falling limply from her hand. She picked it back up, and walked back into Charles' room, where she continued dusting.

By the time Nelly Harrison had moved to the windows and was beating the red curtains, flaying them to eradicate the grime, she saw a speck moving in the fields beneath her. Polly was advancing down the valley, in borrowed Wellington boots. There was nothing to Hartlands other than the walking, and she might as well get used to it, these long weekdays when Charles was away in London, earning their keep.

Nelly Harrison had only been to London once before, to see a show with her sister, before she had passed away. It had awed her, cowed her, and she did not want to return there. She thought of

Charles, and how he could spend weeks, oh weeks there, and not return to Hartlands, when she had made his favourite, the duck, again, and it would not do to freeze it. Sometimes she felt a little cross with him for it, but he had to work, and he had to keep Hartlands, but keep from it too, with all those memories of the dark, happy little boy, and his mother, so full of perfect life.

But there were lots of walks around Hartlands, and Polly would be the type to enjoy them, surely. Nelly Harrison never really walked much herself, it seemed to her a leisurely thing to do, and to lack any purpose.

The cleaning was done by midday. Fifteen years ago, it used to take her a full two days, sometimes three. But most of the rooms were empty now, and she only lightly went over the snug and Polly's bedroom, where her clothes still sat in the suitcase, just her pyjamas folded neatly on the bed.

Nelly Harrison would then sit in the kitchen, drink some tea, and make herself some food. She brought sausages with her, from the local butcher's. She thought of Polly for a second, outside in the comforting folds of the valley, surveying what was hers. But Hartlands really belonged to Nelly, she had been there as long as Charles, if not longer.

She settled herself down in the kitchen and, having eaten her lunch, she fell into a deep and luxurious sleep, aided by the delightful warmth of the AGA.

Polly came back to find Nelly Harrison asleep in the kitchen, her head nodding back, nodded off, her eagle eyes shut, blind to the world around her. Polly was glad. She walked back out of the kitchen, out around the side of the house, and broke back into the white room. Nelly Harrison had evidently been there too. It stank of cheap polish, insulting Polly's nostrils with their sense of dignity and order.

She had enjoyed her walk, but the Wellington boots were a size too small, and had left her feet already rubbing red with blisters on her big toe, her little toe and her heel. It seemed insulting to lift her dirty feet up onto the white couch, but she did so anyway, thinking of Nelly Harrison dropping off downstairs in the kitchen. Here, she could wait, and be the jewel of Hartlands, relaxed and reclined, waiting for Charles to return.

CHAPTER SEVEN

Nelly Harrison did not come to Hartlands every·day, so Polly spent Tuesday alone. She found herself walking listlessly about the house, eating little, there was nothing in the fridge.

The thought had struck her that she might walk to town, along the main road, and catch a bus, or something like that. But Polly had never caught a bus before, and besides, she was sure to see someone she knew, whether it was those gossipy vultures who claimed acquaintance with her mother, or worst of all, her mother herself. After their last disastrous phone call, there was nothing that she could say to her now. And Polly's new life did not involve anybody else: not her mother, nor any of her old university friends. They wouldn't understand Charles, or Hartlands, and what she was having to endure in order to claim the house as her own.

Nelly Harrison returned on Wednesday to dust, to spread polish and a bit of bleach about the place. Polly would then go and walk, then return to find Nelly Harrison asleep in the kitchen. She would then retreat to the white room, and sit, and contemplate, and begin to dream. It was in here that she spent most of her time. When it was overcast, and raining, for it had turned to August now, and August is always the most disappointing of all the months, Polly sat in her buckled trench coat, enjoying the views of the valley.

She did not enjoy it so much when the night drew on. Nelly Harrison usually left after she had woken up from her nap, and then Polly was truly alone. As there was no electric light in the white room, Polly had to return down into the depths of the house.

Polly was less of a resourceful heroine, and more of a decorative one. Hence she did not think to change the lightbulb in the white room. And so she would dread creeping back down into the basement at night, because the night brought festering paranoia with the dipping of the sun, which disappeared all too quickly behind the firs and the monkey puzzle trees. Polly, who was so poised, had learnt to be fearful, as she sat in the dungeon of the kitchen with the night and the earth pressing all around her.

Fear, as persistent as a military tattoo, beat at her heart, making her flinch at every sound that echoed about the old house. It could be a million and one things. Bats, mice, rats as big as terriers, the folds of the wallpaper upstairs finally ripping themselves free from their squalid bonds.

Polly would chastise herself, and try to face the terror that lurked unknown in the darkness, but it was no use. There were the squatters that might descend on the place, the not so gentlemanly tramps armed with broken bottles, the proper, dedicated burglars with all the tools of the trade, round the back of the head with a hammer, as quick as you like. Polly lying in a pool of her own blood, billowing into the flagstones, a little quiver still there at her pulse, maybe she would wake up, but nobody would find her in time. Morning would come, and Nelly Harrison would stumble upon her body with the blood all drained out of her veins, as pale and as dreadful in death, as she had been pale and dreadful in life.

They always ran like that, her thoughts, but her thoughts were the loudest and purest things at Hartlands, since nothing else existed there but dust.

Charles had laughed at her when she had wondered about the Internet.

"Dial up, is it still?" Polly asked, looking knowing.

It must have been at some point during their honeymoon in Spain, all those weeks ago, the heavy barrier of time coming up and between them, making Charles' words seem strange and warped. Sometimes Polly thought that she had even forgotten the conversation at the Radisson, and the deal that had been struck between them: him, the kind philanthropist, her, the willing beneficiary. But ultimately she found that conversation impossible to forget.

"Hartlands has never had Internet, do you think it would suit it? The squealing of dial up? Screaming through the house? No, I don't think it would suit the place, do you?"

"Wifi would be quieter," Polly admitted.

"I thought you were charmed by my being not of this century, how you thought I had a 1950s charm. I think those were your words, at least?"

She remembered now, how he had dismissed her so easily at the Radisson, swiping her away with the roll of his ringed hand, which he had kept melded to his whisky glass.

"What is it about me, that you came here for?"

He held her stare as he might have held her face in his hands, gently, with a taut, rough, undercurrent of determination.

"You're something a little like perfection," Polly replied, with an abrupt glance across to the couple closest to them, sat up at the bar, who had probably assumed that they were father and daughter, enjoying this special day of celebration, so intimate, so sweet, so together.

"You don't say you're attracted to me?" Charles laughed, bearing his lips to show his perfect white teeth, stately and all in a line, waiting to gobble her up.

Polly felt that he was teasing her this time, and swallowed down all of her doubts.

"You remind me of a polished gentleman from the 1950s, and I don't think you understand how completely refreshing that is to me, so completely refreshing. I don't want attraction to convolute what we have, but if you want to me to say that I am attracted to you, I will."

If she had been a 1950s housewife to his dapper 1950s gentleman she might have had more technology than she had now, Polly mused, as she sat in the kitchen, pining for a radio with which to hide the din of her thoughts.

She wondered how long she could bear it, whether she could endure living like this for the rest of her life. But Charles would change, she would make him change. She was Polly still, and she was strong, in spite of everything. A few nightmare fears sat lurking in the basement were nothing, absolutely nothing, to her.

The gravel crunched outside. Polly jumped. Fear bit into her like the sharp attack of an angry cobra; she could feel its venom seething through her veins. There would be an explanation, there would always be an explanation. Still, her fingers were trembling and she could not make them stop. She thought of Charles' whisky, or the port he kept stashed away. They might lull her to sleep, because she did not sleep much in her cell-like room with its sagging single bed.

She would lie in the half dark, without curtains to obscure the narrow high windows up above her, and think of the life before, and the life that was yet to come. She did not dwell on the present. It was not fair to her. But the future outweighed the past, it always did. She would not admit to herself yet that she had made a mistake in coming to Hartlands.

The twilight of the room oppressed her; Polly would have preferred to sleep in unrefined darkness. For she could see all sorts of outlines and shadows that somehow resembled people, leaning and leering over her, every time she opened her eyes. She could not make them stop, and then she would plunge into a half kind of sleep, plagued by vivid waking dreams, the water crashing down the river back outside the Radisson. She could not make it stop, the clammy hand at her chest, the deafening blood drumming in her ears. Then she thought there were other people, more people, swarming about outside, in the house, in the snug, in the kitchen. It sounded like they had got the television working, or they were having a cocktail party without her.

Polly would wake up early, because the daylight would filter in through the windows, those windows that were too far up to ever think of hanging curtains over them. Then the fears would dissipate, and she would push open the door to the snug, and walk up into the kitchen, and no one would be there, if Nelly Harrison had the day off. And if it was not Nelly Harrison's day, Polly would go upstairs, and luxuriate in Charles' bathroom, feeling clean and cleansed from all the terrors of the night.

It was a Friday afternoon, and overcast. Polly sat in the white room in her coat, meditating on the room. It was one of her favourite exercises. Nelly Harrison had been in earlier, with the cooked duck, ready for Charles' return. She had not said anything about all

Polly's uneaten meals, left to moulder in the fridge. She thought perhaps that Polly did not eat by choice, emulating the heroine chic of the 1990s that Pauline had attempted, although she admittedly enjoyed the heroine more than her endeavour to lose weight. And Polly did not really eat any more, apart from the noodles and the custard creams she had found stashed away at the back of a cupboard.

The breeze blew in a little chilly from the open window, and Polly shivered.

She had taught herself to plan, but in order to plan she had to ponder on what had been. Today, as always, her memories fluttered and congealed around her meeting with Charles at the Radisson. She would make it move her forward, though, however much he would try to drag her back.

"Your release, Polly, your release," he murmured, rotating the idea of her ultimate pleasure around in his grey tired mind.

She was beginning to think that those few whiskies had made him drunk. But Charles was in command still, his language pure, although his thoughts were disturbing and cruel.

"You standing there in the night, the fools stumbling around you, stumbling home, stumbling to feast on chips and pizza, but you standing there under the streetlights, stained all yellow," he paused, letting his eyes roll all over her body, "how funny that your pleasure should be of the night."

Polly had pondered then whether or not he was being lewd, and she wondered now, as she felt his gaze grow over her again.

She paused, deliberating if she had to flirt to try to keep him musing, and amused.

"Don't be lecherous," she teased, across the marble table.

"I'm not," he replied, admonishing her playful tone with something darker, a black coffee, which he then ordered. "I'm never lecherous, or lewd."

He paused again, watching with appreciation as the waiter silently placed the coffee on the marble table.

"But you're not really a creature of the night, are you, Polly? I think you're something altogether more black."

Polly felt the pungent potent suggestibility of his words. They had jarred her then, and they jarred with the white room in which she sat now. But now she was planning, planning and ordering and taking back her life.

She guessed he must want her, if only a little bit. And it would make it all a bit more bearable if he could just give into and admit his want, so he would not be so superior and so very deadly. Polly would bring him down to the earthly level he must surely crave. He must surely desire her, he who had said that she was so beautiful.

If she could just but control him, she could then control Hartlands, and it would all be hers. She could get rid of Nelly Harrison and the duck in orange, and dress up those empty sad rooms, returning them to something like their former splendour.

All she had to do was to make him want her, and to make him give into the darkness in her soul of which they were both so doubly afraid. But the purity of the white room did nothing to help her, as she thought about the seduction and how it might be done.

But Polly had seen it done before, many times, played out upon the blank canvass of her housemates' messy emotions. And in her former life, seduction went hand in hand with alcohol. They were veritable bosom buddies, as they worked together to decrease self-control and to abandon restraint. It was an easily repeated formula, a science, something that Polly had always held herself aloof from.

Because, although the alcohol did most of the seduction work, she knew that there were these things, underlying desires, passions of the flesh, which were also flung into this heady and volatile mix. Polly did not understand them, how could she, when she had never felt them before.

But crucially she knew how her friends went about the business of seduction, flirting with flicking eyelashes, showing a bit of flesh, flashing their full red lips. And so Polly guessed what she must do. She held on tight to the night when he must surely return and rampage through the duck in orange, and sip at the port to transport himself away from London and the rattling drone of his academic life, buried deep beneath the dust of the thoughts of ancient minds.

She slipped down into the basement earlier than usual. She went to her suitcase, and picked out a black dress, bringing it up over her head. It was dramatic, exhibiting her skin in its white luminosity and pale vulnerability. She tied up her hair, put on a little maroon cardigan, and waited. Presently she heard a car gnawing at the gravel outside. A spark flashed within her, and she knew what she must do.

Charles had no words for her, only for the duck in orange. He asked her to heat it up for him, and Polly did as she was told.

"How's the university? Is it busy, in the holidays?" she asked, carelessly, as if her words to him meant nothing.

Her cheeks were brighter, and her eyes shone, as she tried to interrogate him. She was beginning to feel alive, like she had escaped out of the torpid stupor she had been wading through whilst Charles was away.

"Research, Polly, I have research to do. You needn't sound so suspicious, like a needy, nagging, wife."

"You might have called."

"You're doing a good impression of one, certainly," he sneered. "I thought better of you, Polly, I really did."

"Although I admit I have nothing to receive the call on," Polly pondered, bending down to check the progress of the duck in the AGA, "it's quite dangerous, really, think if there was an emergency, or an intruder?"

She paused, and made him look at her.

"I might die," she drawled out, finally, spinning from the AGA that had held her gaze, warming her face as she watched the duck in its sauce, which popped about madly now as it boiled.

"Don't be hysterical."

"Shan't you ask me about my week?" Polly asked, some pertness in her voice, as she sat down at the table.

She held in her hands a bottle of port, and she poured it tumbling into Charles' glass.

"I didn't ask for port."

"Like you didn't ask me about my week, here, all by myself."

"You had Nelly Harrison."

"Of course, Nelly Harrison, I had forgotten," Polly said, lazily, smiling slightly, as she picked up his glass and drank his port.

She stared at him, as he looked back at her.

"You're disgusting, Polly, you're not what I thought you were," he shot back, almost stammering as he did so, to see her, so attractive, leaning across the table and wetting her lips with the dark red sheen of the port.

"I've been awfully decorative all week, I hope you'll be proud of me. I opened up the white room, I hope you don't mind, but it's the best place to be ornamental in, I'm sure you'll agree. Well you will agree, I've done nothing to flout our deal."

She sipped at the port again, a big, luxurious, sip, and looked at him steadily from across the table.

The port burned her throat, but she hid her discomfort and continued to hold his gaze. The room was silent, and she could hear his breaths, coming fast and deep across the table. It was so easy, surprisingly so. But it was as she had planned all afternoon in the white room.

Polly began to play with her hair, twisting it into a ringlet with her index finger. She watched him as he ate his duck. She told him that she was not hungry, and it was true. She was not hungry. The port had fired something in her stomach, she felt lighter, freer, somehow. And she knew that she did not really disgust him, as he concentrated on tearing through the sinews of the duck.

"Remember, at the Radisson, I told you about my crush on you, and you were surprised, considering that we were going to be married, man and wife. Did you return the compliment?"

Charles stared across the table at her.

"You remember that conversation still?"

She nodded.

"Well, I remember the first thing I said to you was that you were beautiful, more beautiful than I could have ever expected or imagined. But I don't know why I'm telling you this, you've heard it all before. You're just greedy for compliments tonight, Polly."

Polly nodded again.

Charles finished his dinner and went back up the stairs, leaving Polly alone in the dim kitchen. He had almost run away from her. It was like she could not be controlled, no, not any longer. In her solitude she had gathered strength, and the spirit of Hartlands had eddied into her veins.

Charles had always known that the house needed her, but perhaps he did not appreciate quite how much she needed the house. This last week she had transformed into a creature who finally had flesh and blood, and he could see the red blood beating at her cheeks in a way that he had never noticed before. She had been a china doll, an ornament, a feast for his eyes to savour. He was not tempted to touch her like that. He could fulfil his role as a philanthropist and bequeath her this place. He would not give her his heart, or let her see his need.

When Charles got to his room he shut the door, drawing the flimsy little bolt across it, as if he could keep the new Polly out and away from him.

Ten minutes later and there was a knock at the door. Charles waited a second, deliberating. He knew it could only be Polly, and he guessed that she must have followed him up the stairs.

Slowly, he opened the door, bracing himself for the inevitable.

"Charles, I'm sorry," Polly said, a shaft of light raining into the dim corridor and illuminating her pale skin and dark hair, "I'm so sorry. I know what you said, I really do. But I just can't help it, I can't."

She was wearing her white silk dressing gown, and not much else. Charles could not tell. Something rose up in his veins, his breathing came quicker, he would not, he could not look at her in her pale fleshiness.

And of course, he knew what he had said. He was world weary. He had liked that phrase. It spoke of an experienced ennui, a dignified torpor into which he could slip, older, knowing and replete.

"I just want to observe beauty now, look at it, and I'll do that to you, Polly. I'll observe you, you in your frame, down at Hartlands."

He felt himself speak those words, and he was struck by how cavalier he had been, how cruel he had been to her at the Radisson, her in her red dress, so charming, so intoxicating, so dignified.

"Can I come in, then?" Polly breathed, the dim light softening her harsh beauty, as she stood in the hallway outside.

"Can I?" she asked again, seeing that Charles was aflame with indecision.

She placed her hand, with its long fingers, onto Charles' chest, and pushed him back into his room. With a slight shudder, she felt that she had become monstrous. She would pin him down onto the bed, and throw off his clothes like she was restyling a shop window dummy. She would destroy Charles, and tame him to her will. It was the only way.

Polly advanced into the light. Charles could see that she had painted her lips red, and that she wore a hint of make up, dark kohl under eyes, stretching with a little cat's flick beyond the sockets. She breathed out a dark sensuousness that he could not possibly now ignore, as she sat down upon the bed, his bed, and crossed her long bare legs, staring at him from across the room.

"I'm sorry I came up here, Charles," she smiled, in a measured, calculating, fashion, making him watch her open mouth, as she pushed some nervous breathy laughter from it, her white teeth gleaming in the faint glow of the bedside lamp.

"Are you drunk?" he asked, because he felt it now, and his control was slipping away from him like the turning of the tide.

He paced the room in front of her, trying to avoid her gaze.

"Perhaps, but I've never been drunk before, so how would I know what it was like?" Polly pondered, languidly.

She wondered if he could penetrate the fearful confusion behind her polished veneer, her white dressing gown and her long pale limbs. Whatever happened, she could not allow the mask to slip, not when she was so close. So she stretched out on the bed, his bed, lying back slightly upon the plump cushions.

"I think you should go now, I really do," Charles commanded, his voice cracking slightly as he paced the room again, "you've seen where I sleep, Polly, and that's enough, it really is enough. You need to leave me alone now."

He ran his hand through his hair. Polly could see that he was shaking, and she laughed.

"Make me," she drawled afresh, giggling at the seductress she was trying to be.

It was really so very funny, after all. She, Polly, who was cold to the core, trying to seduce a man. A man she had married to boot, to have and to hold although he would never hold her, for she was his exclusive piece of art. It was ludicrous, and she giggled afresh, letting down her dark hair with a voluptuous plunge, so that it mingled merrily on her white shoulders.

Charles advanced to the top of the bed, where she lay. Polly sat up, drawing herself onto her knees so that she unavoidably intruded into his eye level. There, as she had done in the London flat, she ran her hands down his neck, stroking his cheek and its faint flicker of stubble. She pressed her lips to his and, after a moment or so, of agonising deliberation, he responded, pressing his lips to hers in a fervour, pushing her down onto the bed and ripping off the dressing gown in a mania, like he was a man possessed. He was kissing her, stripping her, pushing her back down, all in one fervid movement, all the while trying to take off his own shirt and his shoes, which clunked down heavily onto the wooden floor beneath him.

Polly could not all of a sudden control him. She became frightened of his mania, as he ran his shaking hands down, down her body, down her thighs, kissing her as if he would devour her. She shivered. He must have felt it. But he continued, nevertheless, half out of his shirt, one sock off, his jacket crumpled on the floor.

She was not kissing him back now. She lay, disgusted under him, the mask uncovered, the mirror cracked, her eyelashes twitching in pain.

After a while, he noticed it. He flipped out of his sensuous frenzy, dragging her up off the pillows, digging his fingers into the scanty flesh of her shoulders. She felt like a corpse to his touch.

"You bitch!" he cried, his chest heaving as he heaved her off the bed and onto the floor below.

Polly's skull smashed onto the hard floorboards as he tried to cast the demon out of her, and the demon out of him.

"You bitch," he cried, brokenly, as he stood above her prone body, "I am right, I was right. You don't feel. You aren't able to. And you tried to trick me, to cheat me, to conquer me, to make me take back my words, but I will never take them back, and you will never win."

He was panting now, his skin scarlet as he bent down over her to inspect his handiwork.

Polly lay with her eyes half closed, her head throbbing, Charles shouting on top of her. She felt his breath encroaching, sliding against her cold skin, the same skin he had just been ravaging with his kisses.

"You don't want me," he was muttering now, "and you never did. You just seek to play me, don't you, Polly? Don't you?"

His mouth was vile as he pressed it against her, bending over her, bending down into her, his hand on her stomach, pressing her into the ground.

"You want to test me, am I right? To see if I am so world weary as I say, to test our agreement made at the Radisson? Am I right? Tell me, am I right?"

His voice suddenly became piercing; it cracked and shattered as it moved across the room.

"You're right," Polly said, simply.

The pain was flooding her head, and her eyes swam with the confused image of Charles on top of her, pressing his hands into her stomach. She suddenly became afraid that he was going to push right through her, it felt like her ribs were cracking and that her spine was breaking. But the more he hurt her, the more her resistance rose.

"Although you could just pretend that I was Pauline, couldn't you?"

The voice was not her own. The jaw upon which his hand came crashing down, however, most certainly belonged to her. Then he went for the other side, and hit her cheek. The pain was searing. She opened her mouth and blood came out of it.

He was not on top of her any more, pushing her, eradicating her into the floorboards, brushing her away like Nelly Harrison chased the dirt with her feather duster. He was somewhere else in the room now; Polly had the distracted sense that he was pacing again.

She shivered. The back of head responded, a dim echo of the pain that throbbed through her like a bass beat back at the club. Her jaw ached monstrously, and her eye sang out in an exquisite misery of teary aggravation.

She slid her hand up to her mouth, and felt where the blood poured out from it. Wildly, she hoped that she had not lost a tooth. He could not take a tooth away from her, that would not be fair.

The pain swum around her head again and she felt like she was floating, floating into the cavernous dark where there would be no more pain, disappearing into the shadow of death where the shapes and shades loomed tall above her, placing her into a box-like coffin deep in the earth below.

CHAPTER EIGHT

Every morning after that August night Polly awoke and opened her mouth wide, straining at her reflection in the little travel mirror she kept beside her bed. She had not lost a tooth, after all.

She would then check on the progress of her black eye. It had raged in purple, bitter and throbbing. Polly did not trouble to hide it from Nelly Harrison. Let her stare. And as the days went on it retreated from its rich purple hues, coloured like a bishop's cloak, and instead, putrefied into yellow, a sad mouldy yellow, that hung and clung about her pale face and made her look wretched and ill.

Satisfied, Polly would then feel her chin, running her hands down her neck, to check whether there was a trail of dark blood caked onto her skin.

It had been all across her bedlinen, her pillow and the quilt. She did not know how she had survived the night. When she woke up she thought that she had been murdered, and had now returned as some spirit, ready to haunt Charles in her desperate search for vengeance. But then she could feel it, the blood, dried onto her skin. She peered into the mirror, and she looked more of a monster than a ghoul. And she was cold, very cold, she looked down her body and realised that she was naked.

With some force of will Polly dragged herself to the shower. Today she needed the calm reassurance of the warm water. But it spat back at her, unnaturally cold. Vaguely, she cursed it, but she did not have the energy to resist it. So she stood unflinchingly under the freezing water, as it stung her already stinging scalp, and mingled with her blood in that strange way that blood and water do mingle, lifting it off her skin with caressing ease, and floating with it down her body in streams of dusky red, like the red she had worn at the Radisson.

He was in the kitchen when she got out of the shower. She had not thought that he would be there.

She was wrapped in the brown towel that had been provided for her exclusive use. It was completely inadequate for her long body, hardly covering her. But Polly did not care. With her long hair hanging dankly down the sides of her face in heavy wet strands, her black eye bulging, and her skin tinged a frigid blue, she knew she looked a fright. So she hoped that Charles, sat there with some buttered toast and a smell of burnt breadcrumbs that suffocated her, might have been frightened and appalled by her appearance, flummoxed into guilty contrition. But he took a bite of the toast and watched her curiously as she tiptoed across the flagstones, dripping slightly as she went.

"Careful not to slip," he drawled, returning his attention to the newspaper at his side.

Polly did not see him for the rest of the day, nor the day after that. She assumed he had gone back to London, now that he was finished with his business down at Hartlands.

In an extended type of daze, Polly retreated to the white room, hoping that she would feel safe there. And soon the days got muddled, and she realised that Charles was right, Hartlands was timeless. It did not really need time, especially in the white room, where she felt so close to the subtle changes of the seasons, the gradual slide into autumn, the coming of the freshness that she relished. All the days were the same, each one overcast like the last, and soon Polly thought that it had begun to feel like September.

But Polly could not tell for how long Charles had been gone, nor did she know that it was August still. For Hartlands had begun to sustain her, and as she sat in the white room, gazing away at the days, she had no need of anything or anyone else. Yes, he had beaten her, and yes, she was cowed. But her resistance trembled still, flickering under the bruises around her eyes, and she remained intent on bringing him back down to her level, the level that belonged to the bruised and the damned.

Polly might have sat like that for days or weeks, as the fog of abuse that hung around her like a deadly mustard gas faded, and the image of Pauline, in her wedding dress that was so like her own, began to conjure in her mind. There was an awful gleeful defiance in the way that she titled her lips to the camera, a gulping sensuousness that was a rallying call to arms. And the only thing that remained of Pauline at Hartlands was her bedroom, to which Polly felt irrevocably drawn, although it was barred to her. But she became resolved to break into it, for that was one way of resisting him, after all, and it seemed like Pauline was egging her on from far away in Argentina.

Polly, with her yellowy black eye, slipped down out of the white room to find Nelly Harrison. She never spoke to Nelly Harrison, and Nelly Harrison did not really ever speak much to her.

A couple of days before, Nelly Harrison had arrived in the kitchen with a bundle of magazines she thought that perhaps Polly might like to read. Polly had laughed in an uncertain way, glaring at the keeper of the house through her painfully narrowed eyes.

Nelly Harrison did not cook the duck in orange any more, and instead brought meals in packets for Polly. Polly sometimes ate them, only if she was really hungry.

And Nelly Harrison never did ask her about the eye, and the blood on the sheets. There was so much silence in the house that it had begun to deafen her. But if Nelly Harrison could keep quiet about Charles Carraway's brutality, then she must also be relied upon to keep quiet about Polly Carraway's insatiable curiosity about her glamorous predecessor, Pauline.

"I want to see the room," Polly began, with some difficulty.

Her lips were dry, and she had not spoken for several days.

"Which room?" Nelly Harrison replied, quickly, putting down her knife and fork next to the remnants of her sausage dinner.

"Pauline's," Polly said softly, with an undertone of authority that made Nelly Harrison get up from her chair, as if she recognised her new feudal lord standing before her.

"Here, take the key," Nelly Harrison replied, delving into the pockets of her loud floral apron, "I don't know why I carry it around really."

Polly smiled, and thanked her in that same soft and direct manner.

She smiled all the more as she went up the servants' stairs and plunged back onto the great yawning landing, drawing her finger along the edge of the long metal key all the while. She might find sustenance from Pauline, she who was mostly likely another victim of Charles' control and devastation.

Polly reached the door and put the key into the lock. It clicked. Nelly Harrison had not tricked her, and without hesitating, she went into the room.

Inside it was just how Pauline must have left it. The blinds were down, but the light struggled, shining, into the room. It created an orange glow, like Polly was looking at a sepia photograph, absorbed by an atmosphere of curious preservation. Some of the drawers of Pauline's white dressing table were open, and assorted bits of lingerie clung like multicoloured limpets to them. And what was most curious of all was that the room was entirely white: from the curtains, to the carpet, and all of the furniture, exactly like Polly's favourite room downstairs.

Polly sat down on the bed, and it puffed dust back at her. She let her fingers rest on the faint lacy pattern on the bedspread. She looked down, and an old corset, besmirched by the dust, lay there crumpled, just next to her feet. Pauline had been a passionate woman, evidently, as Polly surveyed the bits of lacy lingerie that hung from the drawers. It struck her too that Pauline had been in quite a rush to leave this beautiful bedroom.

Polly went to the wardrobe. Some big coats hung there; presumably they were not needed out in the heat of Argentina. She moved one, camel coloured with big shoulder pads, and the moths flew out, gasping and distracted, landing on Polly as they tried to flee from the dust and the cobwebs, the sordid bits and bobs that lay suspended on the floor and dripping out from the drawers. There was nothing from which Polly could gain help, or sustenance, only she knew now that Pauline had been a woman of great passions, and appetites. Her photograph down in the snug had told her that, though.

She went back to the great white bed and sat down on it, the dust nearly choking her, as she decided to lie back on the pillows and try to dream.

Pauline must have provoked great passion and need in him. He had not shaken Polly that night; he had abused Pauline. Polly was not even in the room, she had never been in the room. It was the ghost of this woman, who left dusty trails about her bedroom, clues in big coats and crumpled dirty corsets.

But the room had served to stir Polly back to her purpose. She knew now, without any doubt, that she would have to repeat the whole sordid debacle if she was going to have any chance of bringing her husband under her control, so she could have Hartlands perfectly, and savour it as it ought to be savoured. She longed for it to be cleansed from the threat of his superiority, freed from Nelly Harrison and her narrow eyes and frizzy hair scanning her every movement, and purged from his latent command of her and how she connected with his house, her house.

She lay back, immune to the folds of dust that embraced her like spider's webs. Gratefully, she immersed herself into the soft fabric of the bed that was so unlike her own down in the basement, with the coloured quilt and the dead prison walls.

Polly was tired, she dozed, and finally, she fell into a deep black sleep.

"So, you like it here, then?" Charles said, standing beside the bed with that easy lean grace of his, his grey hair sparkling in the light from the corridor outside.

He stood so naturally there in front of her, although he had been gone for weeks, months, days, Polly did not know. And how he could be so calm when he had caught her lazing in his ex-wife's bed, she did not know either.

She sat up, feeling sick and shocked to the core. She did not dream of facing him like this.

"It is comfortable," she replied, sitting up from the bed and shaking her long hair to rid it from the cloying attentions of the dust.

The air crackled with nauseous energy. Polly would not quite look him in the eye, like she had always done, levelly, questing to match him with her fair and just reason.

"Go on, Polly, look at me," he urged, taking her chin in his hands, "we might as well get it over with."

In his hands her cheeks felt cold and rigid. He took it as a sign of resistance.

"Shan't?" he teased, still with that debonair air of civilised sophistication. "I don't much like being a wife beater, it doesn't suit me. But you see, you've failed me, Polly. You've failed our little promise, our little conversation. You don't look very decorative. You don't look very jewel like. And playing at Miss Havisham does nothing for you, you know."

Polly could feel the bile rising at the pit of her empty stomach. She wished she could be sick, she would be sick all over Charles if she could, the wretched, wretched man, and then he would know what she thought about him.

And like a warning shot, her head began to ache miserably, as if he was slamming her into the floorboards all over again.

"I shouldn't think packet food helps the complexion much," she sadly mused, as if she was lost in a reverie of her own, far away from Charles, who watched her with keen, insistent, eyes.

"You didn't eat the duck."

"I don't like duck," Polly said quietly.

She was still sat on the bed. She fanned out her fingers over the lacy bedspread, casting her eyes over it, as if she could bring him to sit down next to her.

"You never said."

He was watching her as she sat on the bed, but she had turned her face from him. She could not stand to look at him, not when her cheeks stung in anxious anticipation, waiting for the blow of his sleek manicured hands.

"It was not something that was discussed at the Radisson."

Polly spoke slowly, bitterness edging into her voice, as she wondered whether she would enrage him again.

But the man who stood before her was not the pacing, rampaging beast of the man he had been two weeks previously. Now he was poised, poised and calm and charming, standing in the dark room, the door open and a draft wafting in alongside him.

"Polly, let's solve this problem, shall we? You can't sleep in this ghastly room, can you? You need to be safe, treasured. Nell Harrison told me that you've been sitting in the white drawing room. I was glad, glad to hear that. It's the type of place where you belong, not sat up here in this filthy room."

"I don't think you have treasured me though, like you promised you would at the Radisson."

She wondered when Charles was going to pounce on her words, and when the accusations, the anger, the stinging recriminations, would begin. The arguments that had, what did he say? Stained the walls. That must be why Nelly Harrison was always cleaning, trying to sweep her master's guilt away, to bury the bitterness of two marriages, and how many more besides? And the wallpaper too, no wonder it was leaning off the walls, an unwilling witness to all that had been at Hartlands, as it strained to fall down onto the floor, the floor that had been trodden on and abused much like all the Carraway wives.

Then there was Alexander, the little boy, trying to close his ears to the arguments that had closed in all around him, a lurking thunderstorm on a calm purple summer's day. Things never changed, and that was why Hartlands was so timeless: the pair of them, standing in Pauline's room, on the edge of another argument, on the edge of the oblivion that Polly thought she had left behind.

"You don't need to worry about what was said then, Polly," he said, bending down to move a stray dusty strand of hair away from her forehead.

He did not seem riled, angered, or even frustrated by her. He regarded her like an experiment gone wrong, a test subject, which was intriguing and should be documented, not responded to with vital emotions blaring, tears accumulating, the fears growing putrid and the lust rising in his tired veins.

His civil blandness annoyed Polly more than she could possibly express.

"But the packet food?"

It was a weak rejoinder, she knew that, and he walked out of the room, calling back to her as he did so.

"Won't you follow?"

She dragged her feet behind his, knowing that they were about to begin the descent back down and into the kitchen.

"I better get that room locked up again," he mused, as they moved across the landing, "I'll leave a note for Nelly. She doesn't need to clean it though, it can stay like that."

"She doesn't clean Pauline's room anyway," Polly said, regretting the words as soon as they were out of her mouth.

"You really are obsessed with that woman," Charles replied, lightly.

When Polly had uttered Pauline's name before, it was as if she had committed the greatest blasphemy, taking her name in vain like that. It was that lapse that had undoubtedly lured him into violence, and brought the blood billowing out of her mouth. But now it seemed impossible that Charles was the same man, as he remained so cool and calm under fire.

Meanwhile she had followed him to the big door that led back down into the guts of the house, where, to her surprise, he turned round to face her.

"You don't need to come downstairs, Polly, you can sleep in my bedroom tonight."

Polly retreated to the dark of Charles' room. Shocked and surprised that seducing him had been so easy, she bent down to the floor where she had lain those weeks before, cowering and shivering and resisting. She wondered if any trail of the blood he spilt had been left there, but no scar marked the spot, save for a shadow cast by the lamp above her head.

She walked over to his bed and lay down upon it, rigid, wondering how to relax into a more invitingly sensuous attitude. She was unable to do it. All the time she was steeling herself for what was to come, and for what she must do. At any minute, Charles could open the door and slide back into that mad creature of quick ferocious lust and wrath.

Unconsciously, Polly slid her fingers down the cold skin of her neck, feeling for the bloodstains. Time ticked on but she had no way of knowing it. The repulsion grew in her heart, and became the most real thing in the room. For the first time since she had arrived at

Hartlands, she began to wish that she was back in her room in the basement, boxed in like a shoe.

The door clicked open, and light shone in from the landing. Polly lay shrouded in the dark, cold and stiff. Her body defied her; it would not meld its hard lines to become easy and inviting. For her friends, a look was enough, their come-to-bed eyes rotating about the club like a lighthouse. No, Polly would not think about them, not now.

Charles flicked on the main light, and stepped into the room. He shut the door behind him. There was to be no escape, then.

"Well, Polly," he drawled, sitting down on a chair opposite the bed, where he began to ease the leather shoes off his socked feet. "It is what you wanted, isn't it?"

He placed the shoes neatly together, leaning back in the chair and folding his arms as if to observe her better.

Polly said nothing, and lay still on the bed with her eyes shut tight.

"I said, isn't it, Polly?"

"Why am I here?" Polly asked, finally, opening her eyes so that she could see him watching her from across the room.

"It's what you wanted, Polly darling. I know you'd prefer to sleep here rather than down in Nell Harrison's old room."

Polly looked at him, shamed, thinking of the frizzy housekeeper lying in her bed.

"But you can't have it all, you know."

He got up from the chair and fell to unbuttoning his shirt. Polly surveyed his progress across the room like a statue.

"You've not undressed," he said.

"Are you disappointed?" Polly asked, more alert and sitting up on the bed.

"No," he replied, casual and devastating.

"I'll sleep in my clothes, then."

"Good," Charles mused, "you're learning. I suppose Hartlands could be the making of you yet."

Clad only in his shirt, Charles slept beside her, easing into his sleep as he had so comfortably eased out of his clothes. But first of all he had made Polly get up, so they could both clamber down under the covers.

She lay still, prone, listening to his steady breathing, damning his easy conscience that could lull him away into such a quiet and peaceful slumber. Her mind was a mess of confusion: strewn corsets, lost teeth, black skimpy thongs, big purple bruises.

She rolled over and onto her side, considering him, wrapped up beside her in the black blanket of sleep. She bit her lip, rallied herself, and stroked her hand through his hair. He did not wake up; his breath came as steadily as before. Polly then raised herself from her side, and slid herself over him, so that she was couched above him. She hated him most at that moment of his quiet innocent calm.

She took a deep breath; still he had not stirred beneath her. Bringing her lips closer to him, she bent down her head to his, and they quivered. Her breaths came quickly because she was afraid. Then their lips were touching. Polly moved her lifeless hands down his body, to find the warm linen of his shirt, and the warmth of his thighs. She pushed her lips into his, and felt sick.

Suddenly he stirred, and Polly knew he was aroused. She kept above him, pressing her lips into him, holding his name in a whisper between her white teeth.

"Charles," she said, and she felt his eyes flick open.

He was sick with his short deep sleep, and did not understand what was happening, at least, for the moment. Indeed, he almost seemed to respond to Polly's gentle whisper.

"Polly," he echoed, confused only for a second.

He must have thought that it was a dream, but now he had finally woken up. He pushed her off him with a determined action. Fierce yet gentle, he was not the beast of the man he had been before. It was worse though, ten times worse. He was disdainful, hateful, controlled and controlling.

"You won't ever seduce me like that," he scoffed, "in jeans and a t-shirt. Go to sleep, Polly, just go to sleep."

He rolled easily back into his own sleep, and soon Polly could hear his steady breaths. She knew that a sleepless night awaited her. Even in his unconscious state, he was so present, so devastating, she could not relax with him sleeping so calmly there beside her.

She rolled onto her side, facing away from him, gripping tightly onto the side of the bed, as far away as possible from him. His breaths were coming as steady and as slow as before, and as the night wore on they began to seep into the air around her like a poison gas. She could hear it, feel it, clogging up her ears, rolling into her bloodstream.

The hatred seared around her body as one, two, three, he breathed. She wanted to smother him, to stop the beating of his heart, the straining of his lungs. But she knew that even in death, he would have that twinkle of irony in his eyes, that slow laconic smile spread out across his lips. He would manage it, and he would crush her, even then, he would kick her back down.

CHAPTER NINE

As soon as she saw fresh light creeping through the windows, Polly left the room. She went into her little shower downstairs; it fizzled and guzzled the cold water down onto her, but it could not wash away her aggravation with the man upstairs, who could sleep so stilly, like a baby.

She stole out of the house like she could steal away from him. But Hartlands loomed over her eternally, casting its shade through her as she tried to walk away from it.

The fresh morning air did something to revive her, as she chose a track that looped south before coming back round to the north. She had never been on this path that curved so curiously about the estate, and ended abruptly at a wrought-iron gate that seemed to lead to nowhere. She pushed at it. She would know everything about Hartlands, and spite him yet.

He must have told her not to come here, so early on in their young marriage. Admittedly, it was probably not the done thing to send your new bride to the family cemetery, which was carved into this hill before her, all mossy and dank and morbid.

Polly shivered, and sat down on a bench that had been placed to give mourners a better view of the dead. It was so singularly claustrophobic and damp there in the cemetery that had been carved out of the wet earth, with the low stone wall surrounding it, holding back the loamy soil and the dark trees that lurked around the graves like grim portents from the underworld, only their warnings had not been heeded.

Stumbling upon the cemetery on this late summer morning, Polly felt like she had found the hollow soul of Hartlands. But the elaborate headstones, populated with the desperate weeping angels of Victoriana, made Polly feel nothing, apart from the cold. The bright sunlight felt very far away, as if she had fallen into Hades.

As she drew herself up to leave, she noticed the dead leaves around her. They must have fallen from the previous autumn, and they were damp and soggy under her feet.

Polly began to feel threatened by another set of matter decomposing there underneath her shoes – the swarmed mass of the Carraway ancestors – as she gazed at the earth. The skeletal stare of the Carraway patrimony was upon her and there was no escaping them, and their control that they had wrought here down over the centuries. She was just another female staggering under the weight of their history and their power. Polly felt it, and she had to leave the cemetery.

She strode back down into the valley. The sun was beginning to take hold of the cloudy sky, and she felt its warmth with gladness as the rays settled down upon her pale skin.

For the first time in weeks, Polly began to think about her mother. It was funny how she lurked just three or four miles away to the east, cosy in her little cottage up its narrow cobbled street. She would be lunching with her friends, taking tea with Petunia and her new boyfriend, whiling out the long days with bridge sessions or French classes or whatever it was she did to numb the growing bitterness resulting from an amicable divorce.

Polly was almost beginning to forget she had a mother. It was not like they had been close, and it was not like Polly had ever mattered that much to her. It was her stepmother Cassy who had given her cuddles, or at least Cassy had tried to cuddle her, for Polly had made a point of rejecting any tender displays of unwanted affection. It was Cassy who brought her brightly coloured plasters to cover up a grazed knee or a scratched arm, whilst her own mother took no pleasure in the joys of motherhood. It was all so arbitrary, and Polly had imbibed her apathy from a young age.

Then there was her older sister, Petunia, who would scorn her, and belittle every little thing she did. Petunia did everything to perfection, and there was little that Polly could achieve that could be labelled extraordinary. Petunia had been there, and seen to that.

Thus Polly felt like she had never truly mattered to her family. They always had other bits of life to which to attend. Whether it was bridge nights or Erica, her annoying little half-sister, there was always something or someone greater than Polly. It was then little surprise to find that Polly had spent most of her life trying to search for what that exactly was, so she could enjoy it with them too.

And now she had parted ways from them, nailed her colours to the mast, so to speak. She could not return to them now, not now that she was on the brink of something so unimaginable. She would wait for the glory, and bide her time, for there would come a time, surely, when Hartlands would be truly hers.

But Charles continued to baffle her. He made her cook him dinner that evening, and afterwards made her lie next to him like she had done the night before.

"I hope you won't try to touch me again," he said, as he sat at the kitchen table, finishing the duck.

Polly shook her head, watching him dully. She had not eaten dinner, as if through her hunger she could try and protest something to him.

"You need not fear," she offered, as he scraped his plate clean.

"I thought I was being kind, letting you sleep up there. It's not so awfully nice in Nell Harrison's old room."

Polly shook her head again, as mechanically as before.

"It's all part of your philanthropy," she said, toying with the word she had once wished to crush, but now it was bigger than her, and she could not muster enough bitterness to scorn it away with the roll of her tongue.

"You don't understand how far your actions demean you," he explained, placing the knife and fork down together on his empty plate. "Desire is ugly, with you."

"You don't want me."

Polly spoke as if she was resigned to the failure of her plans. If she could not seduce him, there would be no other way in which to control him, as she did not think he possessed another weak spot.

"Not in that way," he sighed, "you should probably go to bed, it's late."

Polly did not know what the time was, but she obeyed him anyway, changing into some soft cotton pyjamas before she went to lie tight and rigid in his bed. He nearly swaggered into the room, giving her a flash of his winning grey smile, before he slowly undressed in front of her.

He said nothing. She kept her eyes shut. He knew she wasn't asleep. She could sense him watching her. He climbed into the bed next to her. She shuddered, in spite of herself. He smiled, she could feel it. The light was turned off and he fell back into his sleep, and the poison in the room grew and groaned throughout the long night.

She was immensely relieved when he left for London the next day, and left her alone at Hartlands. But her peace was always spoiled, and she could never relax, because she knew that he would inevitably come back. Like the nights she spent sleepless beside his unconscious body, she could not rest because his spirit was still there, invisible and yet so very deadly.

Gradually, her logical and rational mind whipped itself into a frenzy of suspicion and hate. She wanted to destroy everything about Charles, but the house she loved was him. What was not his, however, was Pauline's room, for which she still held the key. She would not surrender it to Nelly Harrison, and she had, to that effect, burnt up in the snug fireplace Charles' note to his housekeeper, instructing her to keep that room closed. Polly would be keeping the house now, anyway.

So Polly would slip into Pauline's room with Nelly Harrison's big bucket of cleaning products when the housekeeper had sloped off down the drive and left her nearly alone in the big old house. Every day she would sneak in and attempt to clean it, scything cobweb after cobweb off from the high ceilings, and harvesting piles of dust that leapt up from the pillows and the furniture.

As for the kinky underwear, she picked it up with tongs and let it burn on the fire in the snug. It amused her to see the lacy underwear spit as it was wrenched apart by the flames, collapsing into the blue fire, leaving no traces of the smut that mocked her innocence whenever she used to go into the room and see Pauline's corsets and transparent bras.

As the week progressed, Polly had virtually cleansed the room back to its dazzling white perfection. She had lifted the blinds so that they no longer stained the room sepia, and now all that was left was to bring in the old hoover to guzzle up the dust, which was stubbornly engrained in the old carpet.

It had been some effort lifting the hoover up the stairs. But it was the only purpose Polly had, cleaning this big old room that looked out across the valley, its white folds begging to be returned to purity. Besides, she could not feel Charles in this room. His presence was extinguished; he could not get her here.

Polly dragged the hoover across the floor. It moaned and spat as it went, choking on big lumps of dust and dirt that had accumulated in the years that the room had been so perfectly abandoned. Polly smiled a manic smile as she saw the dust lift off the carpet and its colour change to that of champagne.

When she had finished, Polly sat down on the bed, which was now liberated from the ravishing grasp of the dusty years. She was pleased, for she had accomplished something.

The warm late summer sunlight ebbing through the windows edged Polly to sleep. She had not slept properly for so long, and was lulled into the sweetest daydreams, this room being hers and only hers. But her unconscious bliss was shattered when she found Charles' rough hands on her shoulders, shaking her awake.

"Get up and come downstairs," he ordered, before he marched off briskly.

She listened as he crashed down the stairs and went back below into the kitchen, refusing to open her eyes. But she knew, weakly, that she must follow, and participate once more in his riddling game of control. The thought turned her sick, as the dream she had been living in slid madly into a nightmare from the pit.

Polly reached the kitchen. It was as dim as ever. Two figures sat there, along with Charles, figures that she vaguely recognised and knew she did not want to see. She shrank back a little as their presence sank in. The visitors saw her wince, and almost pitied her, Polly this frightened bird with her feathers all furiously ruffled, cowering in the corner, broken, defeated, tamed.

Charles took in the scene with his cold blue eyes. He would make Polly sing yet.

"Polly, finally! We were wondering where you had got to!" Gabriella cried, in a voice she thought was melodious and embracing, but was in fact grating in its elaborate fakery.

As Polly advanced further into the dim light of the kitchen, Gabriella flicked her sharp dark eyes down over her, and her impossibly thin frame. No pregnancy then, unless she was not showing, but Polly was really as skinny as an ironing board. Gabriella, with her folds of flesh and cleavage one could get lost in, felt superior as the most attractive woman in the room, and turned her ample charms back to Charles.

Her hostess sat, a little ghost, isolated at the end of the table. Polly noticed that Charles had opened some port, and helped herself to a glass. Almost instantly, as she sipped at it, the colour flushed back into her cold cheeks.

The room hushed silent. Gabriella pined for noise and laughter.

"You missed our little dinner, Polly dear, the duck was delicious. Charlie assumed you had gone out."

"Out where?" Polly asked, confused.

"Oh, I don't know, driven off to visit your mother, or something like that," she replied casually, with a flick of her hand. "I think I'm right in saying that she lives in Petworth. It must be nice for you to be so near, and it's such a lovely little town, with all those antique shops. Mike won't let me go there, and besides, what could we take back with us on the plane? Our villa has enough antiquities though, Mike, doesn't it? You're not as young as you used to be!"

Gabriella was guffawing at her own feeble joke and Mike was laughing with her, duty bound as her husband to be amused. Charles raised his eyebrows across the table, joining them laconically with their mirth, and thus the three were united. Polly said nothing, and looked down.

"So, what have you been doing around the place? Any improvements? I thought everywhere looks a bit drab, so different from when Pauline was here. She really commanded Hartlands, didn't she Mike? She didn't let the big old walls get to her, although she was used to big houses, having been brought up in some magnificent pile Hampshire way."

Silence reigned, which Gabriella took as a sign to continue doggedly on.

"It is a shame, it really needs people, this place, Hartlands I mean. It just needs people. You don't really fill the room, do you Polly?"

Gabriella turned a withering eye on the lady of the house, not expecting a reply.

"I'm sorry," Polly said, gulping at the port as if it would magic Gabriella away. "I'm just so sorry to be a disappointment to you."

Mike and Charles exchanged a quick glance across the table. Meanwhile Gabriella was omniscient. Polly must be one of those thin pregnant women who smoke to keep the baby weight down, one reads about them in *The Daily Mail*, or perhaps she practised yoga or pilates, but she didn't look wholesome enough for that. Polly looked like an addict, a disgrace, something Charles was all too aware of. He hadn't wanted to go up and find Polly, but his guests had insisted, and he couldn't hide his wife away in the attic in this day and age.

"When's it due?" Gabriella demanded, determined to have it out now.

Charles rolled his eyes across at Polly, wondering how she would react, the neat little experiment that she was.

"I'm sorry, I don't understand," Polly replied, taking another sip of port, her hands shaking slightly.

It must have been the savage irony, the shame of being a virgin bride, that cut into her, and made her bleed. Gabriella did not notice her pained confusion though, and continued, another of the plagues that Charles had sent down to try his wife.

"I know you're a skinny mini, some men do like that type of thing, and you're probably one of those dreadful girls who care more about their weight than the well-being of the baby. But I mean, is it really fair, smoking and drinking when you're pregnant?"

Polly nearly spat out the port. She suddenly felt all hot and clammy.

"Who says I'm pregnant?"

The disdain in her voice shocked Gabriella, but seemed to please Charles. But still Gabriella was not satisfied.

"Have you not told Charlie yet? I am sorry, I'm such a busybody, poking my nose in where it's not wanted."

Polly looked across at Charlie, who returned her look with that easy ironic gaze, so that she could almost taste his thoughts. She was hardly the jewel of Hartlands now, as she grappled with her guest and was unable to meet Gabriella's impertinence with the refined impatience that was expected of her.

But Polly lacked the delicate touch of the Carraways and their class, who would easily distract Gabriella away from her mighty social blunders, and anaesthetise them for her. Polly knew that she should get up and make the coffee, or find something else to talk about, the weather, perhaps.

Polly knew a lot about the weather here at Hartlands, the subtle changes of the wind, the way the breeze calmed you as you eased into the folds of the valley, and the way it hissed and spat through the firs, chilling its breath through the rows of monkey puzzles.

She must have been thinking, dreaming, filling up the time, clicking down the clock, the clock that was, of course, still trapped at eleven.

"Well, go on then, tell him," Gabriella urged, and Polly knew she could put it off no longer, she was going to have to reply to this blancmange of a woman, a study in vibrant pink, wobbling at her from across the table.

"I'm sorry to disappoint, Gabriella. I am not pregnant. I am, however, tired, so if you'll excuse me, I'll head off to bed now."

"Stay."

She heard Charles' voice sweep across the kitchen. She disregarded it, and turned, ready to head back into the snug.

"Stay," he urged, again.

"I'm tired," Polly said, knowing she sounded like a petulant teenager, or worse, a repetitive drunk, sat outside on some pavement, saying the same thing, again and again. She had heard enough of them whilst she was at university.

"I'm so drunk," Polly said.

She was so mechanically absorbed by her memories that someone else's voice had whizzed out of her mouth. She knew she carried broken bits of speech around with her, and they burdened her, crushed her down, the fragments of conversations better left in the past. But the latent phrases had never taken over her body before, and she felt the words stinging on her tongue.

"I'm sorry," she blinked. "It's not true. I don't know why I said that."

Gabriella and Mike stared at her with astonishment. Mike was looking at her half-drunk glass and pitying her for being such a lightweight, whilst Gabriella began to imagine the empty bottles strewn around where poor Charlie had found her, passed out in a pool of her own vomit. How hard it must be to have an alcoholic for a wife! Especially one that was in such denial. It must be such a burden, what with everything else that had happened during his tragic life.

"Go to bed then," Charles said, so kind and paternal that Polly flinched as she turned towards the snug.

"Hey," Charles called, and she turned back to face him, her eyes wide. "Polly, you silly old thing, remember your room's upstairs now!"

CHAPTER TEN

Somehow the weeks and the days passed, rolling on into October. Charles would come home every weekend like clockwork, and make Polly lie next to him. Term had started now; he had legitimate seminars to run, lectures to give and students to support.

Polly would never sleep, though. The hatred grew up in the air alongside her sleeplessness. And how Charles could sleep when Polly, six inches away, itched to push a pillow into his smug face and have done with it, right there and then? Oh, how she wanted to choke up his airways with white goose feathers, snuffing the life out of him as he slept, unconscious and unable to defend himself. But that was too good for him. He would need to suffer, and not slip off in the grips of a merry dream, in which he dozed, delighted, planning her destruction.

Polly would hate those weekends, and the dread filled up her weekdays. She had nothing to do at Hartlands now she had cleaned up Pauline's room, and so the only entertainment left to her was walking about the estate. Nelly Harrison watched her walk, and she had even given Polly her old Wellington boots, which fitted her young mistress much better than those Charles had loaned her. It was funny, really, that Nelly Harrison had the same size feet as Polly, being a much shorter and plumper woman. But the

Wellington boots were all that Nelly Harrison ever gave Polly, apart from the packet meals and the Weetabix, and the domestic monotony continued.

But after a while Polly found a different way of passing the time and numbing the dread she felt every waking hour. She was never free from the sense that Charles would return any moment to fold her back under his control once more.

Autumn was wrapping itself around Hartlands. Polly felt the chill and relished it. In the foggy October mornings, the white room was colder, unbearably so, but the evenings were warmer, so much warmer, much more delicious and ruby red, fruity and mystic to her tongue.

She had hit upon it that evening when Gabriella and Mike had visited and smirked at her. The liquid she held in her mouth and the way it had burned down her throat had given her a new sense of life. She told herself that it was different to the gin and tonics she had consumed in moderation at university. It was different because the port was vintage and expensive. It cleansed her, it soothed her, and it drew elaborate little fictions out from the walls around her. When she opened the bottle and smelt the rich fruity life within, she knew she had finally conquered it, and Hartlands was all hers at last.

She had found the wine cellar quite by chance when she was poking around in the hallway outside the kitchen. The door was hidden by a row of mouldy old Barbour jackets, festering and damp. She had, of course, promised herself that she would explore every inch of Hartlands, and so she had felt obliged to slip into the darkness beyond the coat rack. Down there, it was truly Narnia: crates and crates of port, vintage port, ruby and tawny and stretching back many years, Charles' liquid wealth, stashed away down amongst the cobwebs, the dust choking the bottles as they lay deep in their slumbers.

Polly ignored the champagne; she had not been able to drink a full glass of it anyway at her graduation. For as she surveyed the bottles, under the dank folds of earth and the single light bulb that fell down swinging from the low ceiling above her, casting flicking shadows about the room, she remembered how the port had broiled around in her stomach the night Gabriella and Mike had visited. How she wanted to feel drunk, just so that she could eradicate them from Hartlands! The ghoulish nightmare that they were. She recalled how she had nearly been transported away by the boiling bubbles of pleasure, which simmered in her empty stomach, but Charles had been there, and he had dragged her back down under the depths of his control. But maybe, maybe if she could drink more, the ecstasy would rise into her mind, and pour a blanket of oblivion over her.

It did. She sat of an evening giggling over the old magazines, the ones that had been accumulating dust, and the ones that Nelly Harrison had so kindly brought to her. She was far away now in a place where nobody could touch her, least of all Charles.

It made her laugh, laugh like she had never laughed before. Hysterical, she had no reserve. She opened her lips and gulped down the air because it was just so splendidly funny. Her stomach heaved, and no, she could not stop it.

So it became easy to forget, now there was just the drink and her spending the night together. It was just so perfect, her and the house and the drink that took away all of her fears.

As she walked about the countryside, the old estate, ranging over the cemetery and the plunging ridge of fir trees, she had something for which she could plan, now she knew she could collapse into a cloud of port and forget. It also gave her something for which to wait. She would while away her days and know what would greet her in the evenings: the flushed embrace of the ruby liquid rising and bringing a desperate red blush to her cheeks.

She must not be an alcoholic because she did not start her mornings with a tipple, or so Polly told herself. No, she started her mornings with a trip to the bathroom to be sick, to purge all of the poison out of her body. Thus the stain of the alcohol would flood out from her system, her head would ache, dizzily, she would then spin around and fall onto the floor. That was how it had felt when Charles had thrown her down from the bed.

Her guts dredged, Polly would begin afresh with a glass of cold water, an even colder shower, and all would be well again. The air would cleanse her, foggy or fresh, she would saunter about the grounds, exploring every little nook and cranny, clambering up to the ridge, running like a lunatic down the lilting valley.

When night closed in Polly needed a little comforting. It began as a glass, and soon a glass was not enough to make the worrying sounds around her ridiculous, to make the nagging thoughts and the bitter recriminations of mistakes and failure dissipate into the night air. Soon she would have to drink half a bottle to rid herself of the horrid reality of the conversation at the Radisson, that conversation in which he had mapped out her future, how she would be his inactive little jewel stowed away in the Sussex countryside.

Polly was not for show. She was part of a private collection, not to be touched, but held in gloves and shined from time to time. And the port made her eyes shine, and her skin shine, shining so painfully she thought she might burn away, spontaneous combustion, leaving only a pile of fluttering ashes behind her as a token of her short existence.

It was November now, although Polly had no way of knowing it. It was Saturday morning, and strangely, she woke up to find herself in Pauline's room. When she got up out of the big white lacy bed, the room span around her. She felt sick, as usual. Despite her growing nausea, she spent several moments trying to understand why she was in Pauline's room, until she recognised that critical moment in which she realised she actually needed to be sick.

Wildly, she ran out of the room, pushing into Charles' clean white bathroom. She did not know or care where he was. Racing with desperate hands to the loo, she tipped up the seat, and gagged.

A burning irony tickled her in the prickly heat that swarmed at the back of her neck, and in the gurgling tattoo that spat vehemently through her veins. Her university friends often spent their time in this way, drinking too much and paying the price for it. And here Polly was now, in the pale magnificence of Hartlands, retching and waiting, retching and waiting, retching and waiting for the climax, as if her stomach might soon burst.

When it came it was pathetic, a little trickle of yellow bile. Polly flushed it away, mildly disgusted, reeling as she always did at the foul acidic burn cloying at her mangled tongue. She felt better, but still not completely well. She turned and retreated to the kitchen, where she sat down, giving herself to the faint dizziness that rattled and caroused between her ears, her mind a vacillating and vacuous space.

She could not seem to remember why she was in Pauline's room, and for that matter, where Charles had got to. She had some vague notion that it was the weekend, and that he should be there at Hartlands with her. But someone had come home last night, when she was sat in the kitchen merrily drinking her port. She had not started her third glass yet, and was glassily watching the static clock and hurling abuse at it for not changing the time, as she knew fully well how the hours ticked away outside.

Outside, she thought she heard the mechanic breaths of a car heaving itself up the drive. She shuddered elaborately, knowing that it was Charles. She took a bigger, more voluptuous gulp of the port. She knew he would ignore her, as he always did. He now treated her with a kind of disgusted amused pity, and drank his whisky away from her in the snug, as she lounged in the kitchen and laughed. How he could ignore her though, his little drunk wife, merry and blithe and so full of life, she did not know. He must have a heart of stone.

"Charles, you look so different!" Polly exclaimed, as a figure advanced into the dim light of the room. "How did you get to be so tall?"

It must be the port, distorting Charles into a finer, younger, man. In fact, he looked so remarkably like the portrait of Alexander Carraway with his wife it was uncanny. The port really did have the most surprising magical powers, having supplied Charles with the gift of eternal youth. Polly giggled. It was such good fun.

"I'm not Charles, I'm afraid. Sorry to disappoint," the figure replied, stepping further into the room so that he now stood directly under the light.

Perhaps it was not the fog of the port tricking her. It must actually be Alexander Carraway stood there before her.

Polly felt him run his eyes down over her body. She had dressed for Charles' return; she was wearing the black dress she had worn when she had tried to seduce him. She was skinnier now though, so frail that under Alexander's intense and knowing stare she might just snap in two. She had to put a belt around the black dress to stop it from looking so much like a bin bag, but it still showed how very thin and fragile she was.

Her hair was down, and she was a pattern of contrasts, a monochrome beauty in the soft light of the kitchen that hid the hollows of her eyes, which gleamed out purple. In spite of her haggardness, the drunkenness that trickled colour into her cheeks and stained her lips a dark seductive red, she was still perfectly exquisite, that ethereal creature she had been in her lacy wedding dress, although now she was something altogether more desperate and alive.

Alexander sensed it, and he felt the air spark between them. He appreciated her, this wild thing drinking expensive vintage port down in the caverns of the house, the house that had always oppressed him when he was growing up.

"Got another glass?"

Polly stood up, reeling slightly as she did so. She had to grip on tight to the oak of the table in order to steady herself. She laughed.

"Of course, Alexander," she replied, obediently going to the cupboards and retrieving a glass for him.

She swayed as she went. It all felt so deliciously bizarre, like a surreal dream, Alexander a floating summer moth trapped down here in the basement, so very far away from the sunlight.

"I'm sorry, you seem to know me, but I regret that I do not know you."

His voice was crisp, she felt Eton all over him.

"You don't have the heavy Spanish accent I was expecting," Polly giggled, involuntarily, as she sipped again at the port.

"Are you disappointed?" he asked, helping himself to a glass of port.

Polly laughed.

"No, I'm Polly, actually," she replied, watching him with deep blue eyes that swam with possibilities.

She was neither there, nor anywhere else. Alexander laughed, but then his face waxed expressionless. Polly did not notice because she could not see him properly, sat so close to him as she was. Clearly though, her name meant nothing to him, but she persisted in presenting it to him anyway.

"I'm Polly," she repeated, sounding out the syllables of her name like she was instructing a slow child.

"Yes, but who are you and what are you doing at Hartlands?"

Alexander did not sound annoyed. Instead, he was intrigued by this young intoxicated woman who had begun to intoxicate him.

"That's a good question, a very good question," Polly mused, daring to look at him now in those brilliant brown eyes, "I married your father."

Polly, hungover and sat at the kitchen table, had begun to see through the mists. She must have started it, surely, it had all begun with her.

He had congratulated her; he had not heard that his father had married again. And Alexander was awed that Charles had caught her, but he had caught Pauline once, not so very long ago. Polly intrigued him, he was not afraid to show it, there was something deliciously unhinged about her that he was drawn to. You had to be insane, after all, to live at Hartlands.

She had suggested that they went upstairs to see his old bedroom, the one that Charles had kept as a shrine. She did not tell him that though, but she guessed that was what Charles would have wanted, Charles who should have been there, Charles who

Alexander had come to see. But Charles must not have come back to Hartlands that night.

Polly thought, moreover, that a walk up the stairs might sober her up. But it was to no avail, and instead she felt more alive than she had ever felt before.

They found themselves standing in Pauline's room. How they got there she could not fathom. But Polly always kept the key with her, for fear that Charles would take the privilege of cleaning the room away from her, if he found out what she had been doing, that was. It was the only thing she could conceal from him, and here she stood now showing it to his son, who ran his eyes over it, over the white folds of the bed and the woman standing next to him.

Polly might have made the first move. She could not break it down and separate the specific from the confused drunken medley of memories from the night before. He was all Latino then, though. All sparkling assault and convenient charm.

"I'm probably not Charles' son. My mother admitted that she does not even know who my father is. There are several candidates, apparently, most of them South American or Spanish. At least that's what she told me on my fifteenth birthday, a couple of months before we left to go to Argentina."

"Charming," Polly laughed quietly, her mirth distilling, as she felt his presence close at her side.

He was taller than Charles, and loomed over her, making her feel small.

"So am I your stepmother then, or not?"

Alexander ignored her, and sat down on the side of the bed, bringing her to sit beside him. Polly felt the room spin slightly, and his touch, fervent and earnest on her cold bare arm, made her feel giddy.

"It made me hate my father, I don't understand why," he continued, delaying the inevitable. "I wanted him to fight for my mother, and fight for me, but I just thought he was fighting against her. Now I think I understand, he must have been fighting for her all along. How could I know that, though? I was only fifteen."

Polly began to think that she must have made the first move. But here was a man who hated Charles just as much as she did! And Polly had never known love, or lust even, but she knew hatred and she gave into it now.

She sighed, a breathy little sigh that made Alexander stop talking so that he looked at her properly, as she sat perched on the bed and gazed directly into his eyes. He drew closer to her, and she felt the madness pumping through her veins, stemming from the fickle mysteries of the bottle. Well, she had woven her own fiction now, as Alexander began to kiss her, her chest, her neck, her hair and finally her lips. She responded, kissing him hungrily, rubbing off the shades of ruby onto his lips. Her eyes were bulging, her heart was pounding, and he held her, tight, so she became a precious little thing in his arms.

Polly had known nothing like this before. He stood up and lifted her, tall and fragile, and threw her down onto the bed. Instead of lying there prone, a lifeless figure, as she had been, a stiff mannequin trying to be sensuous on Charles' bed, she was a picture of perfect longing.

She felt her hands searching for him in the dimness of the room, which was lit only by the light outside in the corridor. She pulled him down on top of her, grabbing at the flesh under his shirt with urgent, greedy, fingers.

A draught shut the door and the room became dark, but Polly was lost in the ravages of an unfamiliar passion, fuelled by the port that flocked through her veins.

She sighed, and grasped at him again, gripping his shirt with shaking hands, it would not come off as quickly as she wanted it too. He smiled, lifted her up from the bed, and drew off her own dress and his shirt in a quick practised motion, his chest slightly hairy, tanned and taut and muscular. Here was a young man, and she pulled him down on top of her again with words she herself did not understand, a steady rumble of ecstatic incoherency, darling, darling, ruin me, darling.

CHAPTER ELEVEN

Polly was still sat in her fuddled state of abstraction down in the kitchen. Alexander must have left when she was asleep, then.

She ached, intolerably, feeling thoroughly miserable. The sex itself she could hardly remember. It had hurt, yet she had wanted him to do it to her anyway. She had dug her nails tight into the flesh of his back as if the act might have taken all her pain away. She had called out his name, not thinking or caring that Charles might hear her. But his car was not on the driveway in the morning, she had gone to the door and looked out for it. So she was alone, quite alone, again.

She got into the shower and there she froze, the water seeping over her skin there where Alexander had trailed his lips, all over his adulterous stepmother. It was so seedy, it was unbearable. Then she heard her own voice of months before, spitting down from the decrepit shower along with the dribbling water.

"And were you safe?" she would always ask her housemates, whenever they came back from one of their nighttime jaunts, coming down the stairs in the morning all green and sickly and proud.

"Were you safe?" she would demand.

And invariably they were. Free birth control and a fear of birth itself combined to make her housemates conscientious about contraception. And of course there was Polly, drumming it into them like a sergeant major.

But Polly last night had not made sure. The port had whisked away all reason and there she was, the arch hypocrite. How prudent she had always been, how bloody scrupulous all the time, and now she had lost her head and slept with her stepson. It was ridiculous, and worst of all, worse than even that, she had not made sure. It was not safe sex, and the urges of a rather overzealous biology teacher came back to her now with intense clarity. Remember, it's not safe sex girls, it's *safer* sex, and the sex last night was in no way safe at all.

Polly quivered at the thought, Alexander's baby, her baby, Charles Carraway's stepson and grandson, all rolled into one.

She continued to shake even after she had got out of the shower and got dressed into her rich purple skirt and white blouse, over which she put a long baggy cardigan. Polly could not stop shivering. She was afraid, she shook for a drink, but she had to deny that particular urge. It was imperative that she could think, so that she could marshal her thoughts into some kind of order, but the fear of the blackness of her situation overwhelmed her. Everything seemed so relentlessly terrible. There was no way that it could be fixed.

She felt the tears eddying down her cheeks, scarring them in their hot manic desperation. She did not know what she was doing as she pulled on a green Barbour jacket from the rack that hung on the wall and shielded her from the cause of her destruction, the wine cellar, and put on the Wellington boots Nelly Harrison had given to her.

She shook all over and still the tears would not stop coming. She wanted her mother. She would go to her. She would understand and pity her. She would know that Alexander Carraway was far more appealing than his father, the professor. Surely Polly would find some comfort there, and she would curl up into a little ball, returned to the womb, under her mother's maternal affection. She would lavish on Polly the love she had held forfeit from her whilst she was growing up.

Polly had to get away and out of the spell of Hartlands. She was slipping all the time into an oblivion, an oblivion that was distinctly out of tune with the harmony of the house.

She struck out onto the drive, and down towards the big gates she had come through all those months ago as Charles Carraway's bride, when she thought naively that she could beat him. But those thoughts were nothing but rubbish now, now that he had won.

As she walked, fleeing like the white-robed woman, she could almost sense the walls of Hartlands falling down around her, the angels weeping at her grave in the cemetery, another poor female destroyed by Hartlands and its wonderful sombre majesty.

Then she heard a car. She heard it long before she saw it, but she decided to steam on, it was all that she could do. Her legs moved of their own accord, and her eyes stung, lashed by both her tears and a westerly wind, which had sprung upon her once she had moved out of the protective shadow of the valley. Her eyes ached miserably, her body ached constantly, and her head swam around in a mess of confusion and fear.

It would be Charles, certainly, and she would have to confess to the baby growing inside her, truer than anything else at Hartlands with its imperious silence and sad empty rooms. To think she had been drawn there, feeling at one with its desolation, like she was another grand object d'art festering its way through modernity. She was nothing better than him, really, at the end of it all, and she had done this to herself.

The car was coming closer, and she listened to its approach with repulsion. She did not know how she was going to face him. She would not even look at it, as it drove past her. Then she heard the note of surprise echoing from its engine as it reversed to chase her back down the drive. She almost picked up her feet quicker, so that she could run and climb over the gate and the cattle grid to freedom.

But Polly did not run, because she was rooted to the spot by the voice that called out to her from the car. She gave up and turned, the ineffable dream of freedom fading as she got back into the car and directed her mother back up to Hartlands.

In the kitchen, Polly brought her mother some coffee. It trembled in her hands. Her cheeks flushed red, as the cold that had bitten at her skin converged with the heat that eddied from the AGA.

"Sugar, I can't remember if you like sugar or not?" Polly asked, more to herself than to her mother.

It hurt her, realising that she could not remember about the sugar. It could, of course, be down to the ravaging effects of her alcohol consumption, but she supposed it was rather due to the ravages of time, and the eternity that had gulped open between herself and the woman who was responsible for bringing her into the world.

She felt a dull ache throb in the pit of her stomach, as if she had been punched, and she sat down uncomfortably opposite her mother.

"So, where's Charles today?" her mother asked, somewhat tentatively.

She was trying to be civilised and polite, playing her role as mother to the lady of the manor, rather than mother to the dishevelled girl who stared back at her without seeing her.

A vacancy shrouded Polly's face. She looked very much like she was trembling, and her mother could no longer ignore her agitated state. Yes, she was still angry with her, livid some might say, and she had, as a kind of coping strategy, built up her own fiction in which Polly resided, blissfully happy, whiling away her days in rural splendour, wanting for nothing. But clearly Polly wanted for something, as she continued to tremble, her wedding ring rattling against the table, her eyes awful, wide and wild.

"I don't know," Polly shrugged, evasively.

Moira steeled herself and took a deep breath. She must forget her anger and her hurt and the speeches she had prepared night and day in order to berate her daughter.

"What's the matter, Polly? Have you had some kind of falling out? Newlyweds do fight, it isn't unheard of. In fact, it was very heard of during my marriage, but you probably know that."

Polly did not answer, and instead she gazed down at the table. A gust of wind blew up against the window, and she shuddered.

"Polly?" her mother began, almost caressingly, as she bit down her anger and her frustration.

Why didn't the girl just spit it out? It was bound to be some stupid row. Why did she always insist on being so sphinx-like? It was so very tedious.

But Polly's attention had drifted, and lulled her back to the previous night, when she had discovered that she was a creature of the flesh after all. Charles had lied to her. She had plunged her nails into Alexander's back with such absolute need, and she had wanted him, she had. But she had to block out the grasping woman she had been, desire was ugly with her, and him too, she had to block Alexander out, as he guzzled kisses on her neck, ruin me, ruin me, darling.

"Stop it," Polly mumbled, completely involuntarily.

"There's no need to be so rude to me, Polly, I'm only trying to help. Will you tell me what's the matter, or do you want me to leave?"

Moira's quick temper had been lit. She had not the patience nor the empathy to stay. And still Polly remained silent, apparently captivated by the sound of the gravel as it clunked together out on the drive.

Like a worried sparrow, Polly looked vaguely about the room. Her instinct was to cower from the door, but she knew that she should try to stand up and greet him. But suddenly, she felt herself too weak to even stand.

"Do you want to get out of here?" Alexander had asked, looking down at her, as they stood in his old room.

He must have been well over six feet tall. Polly was not sure why she should have noticed it then at that exact moment, but he was standing over her now, steadying her shoulders with insistent hands. She did not think to flinch under his touch.

"No," she had said, dizzy with him being so close and with the port that clung to her veins, "I do love it here, honestly."

Alexander looked at her inquisitively, relaxing his grip on her shoulders. He sat down on his old bed with its Manchester United strip.

"It's him then, isn't it?" he asked, sadly, and Polly looked down at the floor.

She should not really be admitting it, least of all to her stepson, but it was him, he was right.

"Forget him, for a night, at least," he urged.

Still she had not spoken, but he took her silence for agreement.

He followed her as she drifted out of the room, onto the landing, and into his mother's old bedroom. She had taken him away from the nostalgia of the Manchester United strip, and the threat of the dark firs craning unseen in at the window, leering luxuriously at them in the cold November breeze.

The door swung open, and his footsteps clattered down the stairs. Polly half rose from the chair, her breath caught in her throat, her hands shaking manically as she clung onto the table for support.

Alarmed, her mother looked towards the door. Polly tried to look in that direction too, but she was trembling, and so nervous that it was absurd. But he would find nothing out. She had nothing to fear. She would scorn him yet.

"Just one night. What's that, when you've got forever with him?" he reasoned, as he held her in his arms and lavished her with kisses.

She seemed distracted, a little dazed to his touch. It was like she was a precious exotic creature brought back from some distant world, abandoned here in this hollow place, with all the bitterness stuck in the walls, the light and the love evaporated from it years ago, if they had ever existed there.

Nobody had ever really loved before at Hartlands. It was family tradition, or a curse. Deadened by arranged marriages, whether the bride was an American heiress or a daughter of the local aristocracy, they were all brought here to languish. She was always stranded, a figure at the window, watching and waiting, observing her new husband out on the hunt, or motoring up to London without her.

But Pauline, Pauline had changed all that, flicking her middle finger up to tradition. She had debauched at Hartlands, she had rolled up the carpets and danced, rolled up joints and laughed. And when Charles had tried to stop her, him the pale imitation of patriarchs past, the diluted phantom of the fading phallocracy, she had laughed at his impotence.

Alexander was proud of his mother, and he would teach Polly to laugh, yet.

"I think this place is forever," Polly had replied, musing in her drunkenness.

Something unknown had stirred within her, as she surrendered to the caressing touch of his fingers. It was how you treated a jewel, after all.

"It will get us in the end, though."

But now she had forgotten death as he continued to hold her. She had ceased to be Charles' debauched experiment, languishing away at Hartlands, her only glory being the woman who had inspired that nice, neat, paragraph in one of the critical quarterlies.

"Who's this?"

A figure advanced into the kitchen, gesturing with a flick of his silver head towards Moira, who plumped herself up, as much as her chair would allow, like a peacock in full pomp. It was immediately apparent that the two would not get on. But before Moira had a chance to respond to this stranger with his cavalier attitude, he had turned all his attention onto Polly, who trembled anew.

She was leaning on the table with one hand, whilst the other was pressed to her stomach, as if she could try and stop any baby from forming there.

It was strange how it happened. Charles' revenge had taken fifteen years: Alexander and Polly's fifteen minutes. Alexander looked down at her, and pitied her, as she slept. He would have to be going. He was only in England briefly for business, and he was due at Heathrow in a couple of hours, from where he would fly back into the arms of his wife, Rosita.

As he pulled on his clothes he thought of Rosita and how devoted she had always been to him. Although her real passion lay in those wretched polo ponies, he was the only man she could have ever brought herself to love. She was no fool, she knew he strayed, but she was always there when he got back, clucking and fussing over him, and the children.

For one last time he let his hand run down through Polly's hair. Rich and black, it was just like Rosita's. Polly didn't stir; she was in a deep sleep, as the coma of the port unfolded itself over her.

The man, whom Moira took for Charles Carraway, paced about the room.

"A visitor, at Hartlands, Polly? Your own visitor? You might have told me."

It was unmistakably a reprimand. His tone was superior and unbearable. Moira, who had been primed, promptly exploded.

"I am her mother, not just some visitor, I'll have you know," Moira announced imperiously.

A battleship with many campaigns under her belt, she was used to holding the floor, and winning it. For what she lacked in intelligence, she made up in redoubtable strength. She would not be sunk, and would keep on firing at all costs. To this end she levelled her sharp blue eyes onto her target, who had stopped his pacing and now stood opposite her, shepherding Polly on her chair.

"Nevertheless, you had better leave us now. Polly hasn't been very well," he proclaimed, eying Moira with evident dislike.

"I'm sorry, I don't think we've been introduced. I am your mother-in-law, after all, although we must be around the same age."

Moira was steering a steady course. As much as Charles Carraway was infuriating her, she had not yet lapsed into the purple rage that defined her relationship with Polly, no, she was keeping that firmly beneath her hatches.

"I'm Charles Carraway, and I think you must be mistaken in your supposition. I must be at least five years younger than you, and the rest."

"Charles," Polly breathed, in a small weak voice, that was, nonetheless, loud enough to attract her mother's attention and prevent her from giving the rather spirited reply she had been intending to deliver with some relish.

Moira had quickly begun to hate Charles Carraway, and she could sense that the feeling was mutual. She was determined to sink him, and polish him off if necessary. She would not be shooed out of this house when something was obviously seriously wrong with her daughter. Polly was sick and she needed her.

"Let me stay, Charles, let me stay here and look after Polly," Moira pleaded, doing the best Mother Theresa impression she could muster on such short notice, "look at her, she's not well. I hardly think these big old walls are doing anything to help her. She needs me. I'm her mother."

"And I'm her husband, and if you're insinuating I'm doing nothing for her care you are much mistaken."

"I want to look after her," Moira returned.

"I'll look after Polly," Charles rejoined, "shall we ask her, is she happy to stay here with me?"

Polly looked up at him with glassy eyes. She had barely been following proceedings, but sensed that the two had been fighting over her. She had never experienced such attention before.

"I will stay at Hartlands," she said, finally, croaking out the words as if they required a huge effort to enunciate.

Cowed, Moira drew in her cannons. She felt herself being almost being pushed up the cold flagstone steps by Charles Carraway. No one could say she hadn't tried. It wasn't her fault that her son-in-law was an odious man, and that her daughter was so perverse. Her daughter. She strained back for one last glimpse of Polly, but Charles was there, a barrier between them, blocking her view.

She stood at the top of the steps now. Charles had overtaken her to open the green door, and suddenly Moira was overcome by a pained sense of regret. She would call out some vague words of comfort to her daughter. But none would come, and Moira stood with her mouth wide open like some dopey basking shark. There was no way that she could fight the deadly sense of oppression that careered into the house with the chill breath of November wind that eddied through the open door. Desperately, she tried to pull the words out of oblivion, to say the things she should have said over the course of many years, but she couldn't, not with Charles Carraway standing there so smug and complete.

She found herself outside, and she noticed that Charles had shut the green door behind them, effectively cutting her off from Polly forever. She looked down to see that Charles had his arm on her sleeve, a truce, maybe.

"This has been going on for some time," Charles began, confidentially, as if he and Moira were the oldest of pals, "and Polly didn't want to worry you about it. I'm sorry you had to see her like that, but she just can't cope with other people in the house."

"But I'm her mother."

"Even still, we need to do everything we possibly can to aid her recovery. She will get better, but she won't get better with these unexpected intrusions, her doctor was very firm about that. She's being cared for by a top London specialist, on Harley Street. You can see that I am providing your daughter with only the very best."

Charles Carraway was very convincing, and he sensed it.

"What's wrong with her?" Moira asked, lowering her voice as if Polly might hear her.

"Personality disorder, nervous complaints, it's a bit of a muddle, but we'll get there."

"Is there anything I can do?"

"For now, go home and try not to worry. I'll let you know if she takes a turn for the worse. But I should think that unlikely, and the next time we meet she'll be as right as rain."

While he spoke, he ushered Moira to her old green Volvo. He had to get her away, this harpy of the oldest school, with her quick indignation and her committed righteousness. She was everything that he despised, and he had to get her off his driveway.

Meanwhile, Moira's mind was caked in confusion. She had come here, she had not known why she had come here, that was right, she was frightened for Polly. Had she said goodbye to Charles? She didn't know what she had said, because the next time she became aware of her surroundings she was thumping back over the cattle grid. But the cattle grid didn't beat any sense back into her, and still the dust did not settle. Marital disputes, trouble in paradise, mental disorders, Charles Carraway, bipolar, wedding photographs, schizophrenia, none of it made any sense.

She got home, back to her little cottage tucked down its charming cobbled street, and the first thing she did was to make a cup of tea. Everything would come right after a nice cup of tea. It was the law of the land. Perhaps she would also have a digestive with it. She needed some blood sugar; she had had quite a shock.

And as the tea seeped into her veins, Moira began to calm down a little. She had always known that there was something not quite right with Polly. She wasn't like other girls, and she most certainly was not like her sister, that paradigm of perfection, Petunia. Perhaps it was better that it had all turned out this way. Certainly, she could not afford for her to be treated on Harley Street, but Charles Carraway could.

Although she hadn't liked him at first, he had grown on her, the way he had spoken about her treatment, he obviously loved her. And Polly's little display, the tears, the sighs, the anguish, that was all part of her disorder. It must be hard on him, but Moira could see how determined he was to make it work. She stifled a little tear, it had crept up on her, and Moira didn't do tears. If only Geoffrey, her ex-husband, had stuck around, and tried to make it work like Charles Carraway was doing now. Only Geoffrey had wanted a younger model, one that submitted to his every will, and Moira wasn't made for submission. It did no good to think about that now, though.

Having drained the cup, with a little sniff of disgust at the digestive crumbs that had made their way into the bottom of her drink, she felt quite restored. She was glad she had visited Polly, and her silence could be explained by her illness. She was most certainly in the right place, with Charles Carraway caring for her and lavishing money on her like she was the Queen of Sheba. No, she wouldn't worry about Polly any more. Polly was safe, and although she was not quite well, she would get better.

Perhaps it was time for a nap, her old green sofa that had been a wedding present from someone, she forgot who it was now, it was so very long ago, was very comfortable, yes, she was very tired, and she would sleep. Perhaps she would dream about Polly, in her very smart kitchen, lady of the manor. Yes, that was perfect, and thus soothed, Moira drifted off to sleep.

CHAPTER TWELVE

Hartlands had, by now, become engulfed by the night. Charles had been absent all day, whilst Polly had inevitably found another bottle of port for herself, and so she was drunk in the kitchen by the time he finally arrived home.

"How could you do this to me, to Hartlands? This is not what we agreed, Polly."

He appeared to be angered by her state of obvious intoxication, rather than by the visit of her mother earlier in the day. It had not gone off too well, and Polly felt bad for her, coming all that way for nothing. But Polly was not really sure what he was so angry about, although if he was upset about her drinking it had taken him long enough to notice. He must be cross because he had finally worked it out, that this was how she was resisting him, this funny man, flapping his arms about him like an exasperated windmill, one tequila, two tequila, three tequila, floor.

His smile was blurred out, if he was even smiling, Polly couldn't tell. There might have been two of him, and two of those irritating smiling slugs that paraded incessantly about on his complacent face. How she had muddled him up with Alexander she did not know.

Now everything else was becoming blurry too, although she could just about make out the smiling slugs, taunting her in their relentlessly smug amusement. She would find the salt and plague him with that, watch him and his slugs shrivel and burst. Although you wouldn't just be able to pick up his mutilated remains with kitchen roll, and shove them into the bin, Charles Carraway's body simply wouldn't fit. Besides, somebody would be bound to ask questions. And Nelly Harrison would know. Nelly Harrison knew everything.

Polly giggled, thinking of Nelly Harrison and the slugs and the shrivelled corpse of her husband.

"It's so much fun," Polly laughed, "and you started it!"

She was thinking of the dirty Martini, go on Polly, try it, live a little.

"I'm living a little," she giggled, bitterly, although she had not much liked the dirty Martini.

Perhaps Charles had thought that she was more sophisticated than she really was. She was not sure. Anything was possible. But she knew that she thought herself very sophisticated then, and above it all, all the violence and sex and death. She used to imagine herself playing the role of some pale goddess, her innocence her repression.

She took another gulp from the port. Perhaps her thoughts would fade away, just like Charles Carraway.

"How many bottles?"

She knew he was shouting now, but she could not see him. Perhaps he was lurking behind her with a meat cleaver. She had never seen a meat cleaver before. She would not know how to recognise it, she would just feel it, yes of course, she would just feel it crashing into the back of her head.

"How many bottles?"

She could not understand his tone, she could not place it. She felt that he could have been angrier, flying at her, smashing her jaw, stealing her teeth. She would not let him take her teeth.

"One," she laughed, "I'm sorry."

She felt like she needed to apologise. It was what her friends at university did a lot when they drank too much. Back then, Polly thought they had a lot to say sorry for, although she wasn't sure why she was apologising to Charles now. Oh yes, he was angry, and if she said sorry, he might go away. But he had done this to her, it was all his fault.

"Polly, there were bottles and bottles of this stuff stacked away, and they're nearly all gone now. But I suppose when they're gone, they're all gone, and that's the best thing for you, at the moment."

Charles was ridiculous, standing there in front of her like that, like he owned the world and everyone in it. But he didn't, and he didn't know what she had done, how she had taken the other bottles up out of the cellar and hidden them away. He thought that she was a crumbling mess, but Polly was always one step ahead of him.

Every day she would take a couple of bottles up to the strange little grotto outside, which she had discovered during the course of one of her many rambles. It lurked up on the ridge, perilously poised on its steep southern edge, which grazed the beginning of the valley. Its entrance faced east, parallel to the precipice and the rising sun.

The grotto itself chilled her; it felt like death. Polly despised it. Its mossy walls were covered with shells, interspersed with little mirrors and bits of coloured glass. She could feel the dead hands picking up the shells on the beach, and placing them here in the grotto. And although the breath of dead men hung there, heavy and loitering, Polly thought that it would make a good place for storing port.

"Polly, I'm worried about you."

He could have meant what he said, but she did not think he did. She had learnt to distrust his parental concern, and she was weary of it. But she still had not drunk enough to forget what had been, and so she was flung back to that time in the hotel bar, where he was telling her that she would be his jewel.

"But I can't be a jewel without it," Polly moaned, her mood changing as the tears gathered in her eyes.

She looked a sight. She was thinner, paler, hollow. Her clothes hung emptily on her, as if the science lab skeleton had been dressed up by the pupils as a prank.

"I may not be a nice man, and I may even be a bad man, but I can still have good intentions."

He was blathering on, a thin speck in her vision.

She started to sob because she could not comprehend it all: his justifications, her bitterness, his endless words, and her hopeless resistance. She had never cried so hard in her life before. She could not understand it.

And the tears kept running, pouring out of her eyes. She thought she was crying blood. But she could taste the salt on her tongue, and she howled on, her lungs ready to burst.

She thought of the river running black under the streetlights next to the Radisson, and how her heels had clicked and rung against the cold metal of the footbridge, as she had walked so confidently across it to meet him. It should have been her fate, flung away down into the weir, a heap of dusky red rags bubbling against the rocks. It would sort the baby out, at least.

Her mother hadn't helped, like Polly hoped she would. But she never helped, and she had walked away, capitulated under the charm of Charles Carraway. Well, she wasn't the first. Or the last.

But besides, how could her mother possibly help her now? It was over, finished.

Polly's tears continued, wrenching at her soul. Perhaps Charles thought she was faking it, like she had faked her lust for him before. But the tears ran on, on and on, filling the kitchen, ringing in his ears, as his wife broke down, and spectacularly crumbled.

"How can I be the jewel of Hartlands when you keep me like this?"

Her voice was unsteady, cracking and fizzing with the steady flow of her violent tears.

He turned on her.

"Me, keep you? I thought Hartlands kept you, you've everything you want and yet you're a crumbling mess."

"I don't crumble," Polly sobbed, a weak little ghost of her former spirited self, "I don't crumble."

But she could not deny that she was a wreck, a sorry bedraggled mess. The tears flowed down her cheeks, her whole body vibrated as she oscillated above the pit, the great pit of darkness, she felt it there, and the oblivion was enticing. No one, no one could save her now, nobody could. Alexander had tried, and he had left her more hollow than she had been before.

Polly had spent ten minutes perhaps, maybe more, sobbing like her soul might burst. Charles had a watch and he looked at it, impatient. He almost preferred it when she had tried to seduce him. Jewels should not cry; she should be poised and perfect. But then, surely, this was what he had wanted all along.

Pauline had intoxicated him. From the moment they first met at a hunt, she wild in her navy blue jacket, the first to jump every fence, him breathless behind her, desperate to catch up, she had seduced him. They had done it in the stables at Hartlands, the stables he had since sold, up on the fields above the valley. She was seventeen, he was seventeen, it was perfect.

Then he went away to university, but she didn't. She went around France, and sent him postcards. They were only little intoxicating messages, daubed with a smudge of her lipstick, containing a vague summary of where she was and what she was doing. But Charles was more concerned over the number of people she was doing. It worried him, so he retaliated, and slept around. And he slept around a lot, boys, girls, he did not think to discriminate. But he hated himself for it every time, and every time he would think of Pauline and the stables, her wonderful black hair, curly and wild, her big passionate eyes and those big red lips. He would try to justify himself; she had her fun and so must he, but still he felt guilty.

So he spent much of his undergraduate life torn between lust and guilt, whilst she alternated her time between being a chalet girl or a tour guide on the Greek islands, leading groups of fat tourists around, and sleeping with the hotter ones. But Charles believed, ultimately, that he had been perfectly loyal to her in spirit, if not in deed. After all, she consumed most of his thoughts, and he sent her detailed letters in tiny writing, including some of the poetry he had been studying at the time, glimpses of Rossetti and Browning and Keats. And she would read the letters, give a full mouthed laugh, and roll over and begin to kiss the man who lay beside her that particular morning.

Polly continued to sob, whilst Charles began to relax, and to enjoy himself rather.

He brought out a chair, and sat down on it. He poured out a little glass of whisky, and watched as his new young wife was ripped apart by her tears.

Of course, Pauline had never really cried, and that was what had made it all so frustrating.

Five years had elapsed after the incident in the barn, and for five years they communicated constantly across the continent. Charles was a Masters student now, but most importantly of all, his father had unexpectedly died, and him being the only child, got all of the Carraway fortune, and Hartlands, of course.

When Pauline heard she came straight back to England on the first available plane, and tumbled into Charles' Oxonian bed. He was overjoyed. His friends were jealous of him for a time, but Charles being a handsome man deserved the beautiful Pauline. And his friends soon grew to like Pauline, however, because Pauline always gave them such sensuous looks whenever Charles went out of the room. She flirted with them, stroked their knees and their egos, and made them laugh. To all of this Charles was mercifully oblivious, but he was to find out soon enough, only after they had taken the serious step of marrying.

But Pauline had never cried like Polly was crying now. Polly had exposed herself as weak, trembling and shaking as she sat there at the table. She had no spirit, none at all, she was so unlike Pauline and her will that could not be tamed.

He had taken Pauline down to Hartlands when he finished his Masters, thinking to have her there to himself. They would while away the summer days before he started his PhD in a frenzied gasp of passion, up in the stables, in the grotto, all over the house. It was like that, so much like that, during the first couple of days. Charles thought he was in heaven.

On the third day, though, she sat rolling a cigarette, her red-painted nails wrapped around the telephone. She was inviting people to stay. From then on, the parties never seemed to stop, beautiful women and handsome men came down, all so dark and enticing. Charles was so English, so decent and sedate, and the worst thing about him, then at least, was his dullness. He treated Pauline so well, too well, like she were queen of the castle. But Pauline did not want to be treated like that. She wanted to be ruined every single night by the spice of the unknown.

He went back to Oxford in order to study. He did have his regrets, leaving her down there at Hartlands, but he thought that if he could just get away, he could at least escape the jealous turmoil in which he had been trapped during the last couple of months. He could never prove anything against her, and she would always smile with that big captivating smile, and swallow him back up again. She knew how he liked it, after all, and she would win, she would always win.

It went on like this between them for several years, and then she got pregnant. Charles was not even sure if it was his, this baby, when it popped out, so dark and swarthy with a headful of black wiry hair. As a member of the landed gentry, that son could never have conceivably been his. But Pauline would say that Alex was her little olive baby, and that he took after her, and not his aristocratic father.

Then the money began to dry up, after he had become a doctor and was trying to make his way in the fusty world of academia. Alex was ten. Pauline was still having parties though, and she was beginning to look a little blowzy. She would smoke weed now to spice Hartlands up, since she didn't have enough money to snort cocaine.

Pauline had never liked Hartlands in the way that she was meant to. Charles hated that about her. And Polly had failed too, she had got drunk, she was always off her face, whilst Pauline was usually high.

Then there were the rows. They had always argued. Pauline was passionate and Charles was stubborn. He was trapped as a man of centuries before, a respectable country gentleman, but then he would always fall back into her arms, into her bed, that delicate white Mecca of lace and lust that was her own bedroom, which gazed out across the valley.

But soon Pauline began to grow so weary of Hartlands that she had to escape from it, now that Charles could no longer fund the parties and the reams of people down from London, the ponies in the stable, and all the nice toys that Alexander should have had. Charles brought him little plastic things instead, dinosaurs, action men, that type of thing, but Pauline thought her son deserved more as the heir of Hartlands. Charles had tried to play with him, but the young boy had shunned him.

He begun to see that he was chasing the impossible. Pauline could never be tamed. Then Alfonso arrived, gleaming from Argentina, all big white smiles and ten years younger than Pauline. This was not just an affair, it was something different, and Charles knew it. Pauline's big white smile would light up the room whenever Alfonso walked in. Then she stopped sleeping with Charles, leaving him bitter and frustrated, and he would shout and rage against her and she would shout and rage back. But it was all so incoherent in those days, he scarcely knew what they were arguing about any more.

Polly sobbed on. He did not know why she cried. Ah yes, perhaps it was the isolation, the isolation of this idyllic spot in the Sussex countryside. So many people would kill for it, he had screamed, and Pauline had screamed back, that she would kill to get out of it!

The babble of their arguments had returned with the babble of Polly's tears, mingling across the table, the confused broken memories of both these wives.

Charles had broken Polly. But he had always intended to do so. He had had years to plot his revenge, years and years. And revenge, what better way to placate the blood lust that burnt up in his veins and made him shake? He would think of it whilst he lectured, whilst he sat on the tube, whilst he lay brewing up in his Islington flat. Yes, Pauline had stolen away in the dead of night with Alfonso and Alexander to get on a plane and disappear far away, but he was going to exact his revenge, and he knew exactly how he was going to do it.

The arguments had at least stopped. Plugged, for now, they hung in the walls, and he could feel them all around him. He started to sell off the furniture. Going to auction was the only way he could get out of the poverty, and besides, he did not want the big dining table, or the ancestors' pictures gazing back at him in his failure to keep a wife. After all, Hartlands had been built on the myth of a raped woman, and he had inexcusably failed the fantasy of female repression that had echoed down to him through the generations. He had failed the Carraway ancestors, and he did not need their trappings any longer.

But still Pauline hung about him, laughing at him, her head tipped back with her red mouth gaping, tempting him, luring him back in. He spent the nights in paroxysms of frustrated lust, ripping the bed sheets beneath him as he thought of her and everything she could do. But she was now with Alfonso. Someone had told him, the infantile Gabriella perhaps, that Alfonso, like a prince from a fairy story, had turned out to be the heir of some great cattle-owning dynasty out on the Pampas. It was then that he sold the stables. He had wanted to pull them down. Every time he saw the little tower with its clock face on the horizon he burnt up in unspeakable lust, only his slowly formulating plans placating him.

His plans were the coolness and the balm that began to ebb through his veins at night. He stopped tearing the bed sheets and pacing the room, as were his monstrous habits in his fiery potent need for Pauline. He became a lizard. The scales grew on his skin, as the plan swarmed through his blood, cooling the lusts, killing the weaknesses in him, and making him forget the greatest love of his life, Pauline.

He continued to sell off little bits and pieces every now and then at auction. He got a job at a London university. The money began to flow in because he was not pouring it down the drain of Pauline's open mouth. He was solvent, once more. He was a normal charming man again. People began to talk to him afresh. He lost that wild, crazed, look in his eyes, and the hollows beneath them.

He wrote books, and had them published. He gave more lectures, and cut a distinguished figure in the world of academia. The books distracted him, but oh how he learnt from them, and Gilbert Osmond became his idol, the great collector, the man who had turned Isabel Archer from the flesh of America back to his cold damp rooms in the ancient darkness of Rome.

He had learnt a lot from his books. It was fifteen years later, and he was ready, no longer a young man singed by the flames of an intoxicating impossible love, flammable and nauseating. He was debonair, the handsome educated man that everybody wanted at their dinner table.

But he did not want to use the Internet to trap her. He had never installed the Internet at Hartlands. It would spoil its peace, and its detachment from the modern world. Instead, it was his little fancy to put the advert in *The Sunday Telegraph* supplement. He knew it was a bit foolish; how many twenty somethings would be looking for love in the pages of a newspaper that spoke of the delights of Saga cruises up the Rhine and the uncomplicated ease of the latest stairlifts?

But then there was a message waiting for him nonetheless, a silly wailing voice down the line, a bit of a giggle, and snap, it was gone. It was probably a joke, but he pursued it anyway. He had not expected Polly to walk into the café so neat and so prim. Here was Pauline: tamed, encased in a demure trench coat, her flesh covered up, not pouring out in low-cut dresses and tiny denim shorts, not fit for the lady of Hartlands.

He liked Polly's conversation, and the way she had looked at Hartlands. She would do, she would fit. He could tame her in the way that he had never been able to tame Pauline. He would not need to touch her, that would certainly not be necessary. He would leave her at Hartlands, and come back whenever he wanted to observe her. He might break her, he had not decided, but he would make sure that he would sketch it all out to her over drinks at the Radisson.

He had been disappointed, however, when she got all fleshy, and tempted him, like Pauline. He was only going to look at her, he had never meant to touch her. He did not mean to get so embroiled in his own revenge. But he had fought back, and flung her down onto the floor like he had so wanted to do to Pauline, only Pauline was stronger than him, and she would just laugh. Pauline was not the type of woman who you could just push down and leave there, and expect never to get up again.

He went away. He had to leave her to see how she would flower by herself at Hartlands. He took her phone charger; she'd be having no riotous parties, no university friends clogging up the place, cavorting through the rooms without care or respect for the magnificence of Hartlands. And she had so wanted to be the jewel of Hartlands! She had so wanted it. He was surprised then when he came back to find her ever more increasingly a blathering mess, dead drunk, or lying in Pauline's bed.

It was ridiculous, imagining she shared an affinity with Pauline. He had to crush it out of her, he had to destroy her, so that ultimately she would sit patiently, a little ghost, and then he would know that he had finally vanquished Pauline, and laid her rebellious spirit to rest in the dank little cemetery that skirted the edge of the estate.

Now she was drunk, and that had surprised him. She was destroying herself; he did not have to do it himself. Of course Pauline had spent a lot of her time drunk, or high, smoking to calm the innate restlessness that tumbled through her veins.

He did not know what to do. He began to feel pity. She thought he had told her everything at the Radisson, of the stillness and the inactivity of her married life. She thought it was all about Hartlands, how Hartlands needed her, and she needed it. Little did she know that it was about killing Pauline.

Polly continued to sob. She was breaking away, crumbling before him with each tear. He looked at it and thought that it was good. Charles stood up, and fetched her another drink.

CHAPTER THIRTEEN

In the morning, Polly did not remember how she had cried. She got drunk the next night, and laughed, but Charles was not there. He had returned to London, apparently.

Polly continued to tell herself that she was doing it to spite him, this drinking business. She looked on it now not just as the only thing that would rescue her, but as the only thing that would annoy Charles, and show him her defiance. If she could not conquer him, she would rebel against his rule.

It did no good, however. He came back the next weekend, just for a night, and made her lie next to him. It was torture to her, but the more she drank the more her sleeplessness dissipated, the white nights froze, and she closed her eyes and submitted to it, floating away into ruby-tinted bliss.

The days grew shorter and the nights grew longer and the monotony multiplied. The weekdays would all blur into one, and every morning when she got up and ran to the loo the questioning silent gaze of Nelly Harrison would beat into her.

Soon she grew tolerant to the port, however, and woke up without a hangover. But it was mechanical, and it always was like clockwork with Polly, she who was so very meticulous. So she would be sick anyway. Besides, she liked the feeling of all the poison dredging out from her, and she would come away feeling purged and cleansed. Her friends had made out that it was painful, hateful, retching away the morning after the night before. But it calmed Polly, and made her forget about the baby, the impossible baby of her night time fears.

It was late November. Nelly Harrison was working that morning, and had watched Polly's little pilgrimage to the loo with sad knowing eyes. She almost felt a twinge of pity, once she realised what Polly had become. But it was not for her to interfere; generations of Nelly Harrisons had swarmed along the corridors of Hartlands and not one of them had thought to question the way things were. Let they who thought themselves to be better get on with it, and destroy themselves. It was nothing to her.

Besides, if her mistress had been a saint, Nelly Harrison would have been desperately bored. She had cousins in Eastbourne to whom she could regale the whole sordid business over Christmas. It made for delicious telling, and the look on their faces! That such intrigue, that such tragedy, that such sin could exist in such a picturesque part of the country, they could not believe, and Nelly Harrison did not wish to disappoint them.

And so Nelly Harrison watched as Polly, up at eight in the morning, punctual to the tick of the frozen kitchen clock, ran into the small shabby bathroom to be sick.

"Anything for breakfast?" she would ask, as Polly came back into the room, pale and a shadow of her former self.

She had always been thin, but now she was positively skeletal as the bones pushed themselves right through her skin. She could be snapped, snapped in two, and that would be the end of the second Mrs Charles Carraway.

"There's Weetabix."

Polly remembered when she had first arrived at Hartlands, and she had asked whether Charles kept a Mrs Danvers. Nelly Harrison was certainly disappointing in the role. Duck in orange was no substitute for envy-inducing tales about the wonderfully beautiful Pauline, or dirty schemes to shame her in front of her husband and the county.

She wondered why Nelly Harrison was being quite so talkative today, and she smiled, oddly. Her facial muscles looked as though they did not want to move, as they remained set, her lips drawn in tightly, as sharp as her jagged cheekbones.

"No, thank you," she said quietly, "I'll make myself some coffee."

She went to the kettle, and filled it with fresh cold water. Suddenly, it became too heavy for her, and her hands buckled. Nelly Harrison watched, but did not help her. Polly did not ask for her help, and watched, curious, as the green metal of the kettle crashed into the sink below, the water swilling out around it. She could not draw her eyes away from the strange spectacle: the kettle lying in the sink, drowning and useless. Eventually, she summoned the strength to pull it back out, and after drying it, she made her coffee.

Afterwards, she cut down the paths that ran northwards behind the house, and down through the fields that pushed away from the dark expanses of Hartlands. She wore the green Barbour jacket, and a grey beanie hat that she had found stuffed away on the rack of dank coats that shrouded the wine cellar from view.

As the cold breeze caught her and made her shiver, she pulled the hat further down over her long black hair. She could have been a shrivelled old woman, her bones thin, her blood thin, her heart thin, as she strode away from the house. The coffee, however, had given her a speck of vitality, as she finally came out of the dark Hartlands woods to emerge into the bright winter sunlight.

As she struck through the fields, the fresh air served to clear the clutter of her confused thoughts. Her mind was clearer than it had been for weeks, months even. She could not rile him, she could not seduce him, she could not be rid of him. But she knew that she must stop drinking; it had not enraged him as it should have done. But she was tired, the ennui had crept back into her soul, and everything seemed so inevitable.

After all, everything was the same at Hartlands. Nothing changed. She never did find her charger, the television did not work, they stopped getting the paper delivered, and Nelly Harrison did not bring it either. She hated it because it was the isolation that Charles had fashioned out for her, not the one she had spied from the copse back when she had failed to glimpse the disaster into which she was about to step.

Had she been left alone how she wanted to be left alone, in charge of the grand property and all its needs, she would have been perfectly happy. But Polly felt more and more that she was nothing more than an experiment, that Charles had no intention of letting her run Hartlands as she wished to run it, that he was never more content than when he saw how incapable she was of ever directing the big old building and its land.

But so complete was Polly's isolation, she did not want to smash back out of it. There was no way she could go back into the world now, the world she had never understood, and had not much wanted to. There was nothing for her out there, out there through the gates and down the main road into Petworth. But Charles, in leaving her here, as cruel as he was, with her body failing and her mind ailing, had imbued her with the greatest gift of them all. She would be separate, finally, but somehow she had to muster her strength to make her escape from the world and everyone in it, and most especially Charles.

She had forgotten that it was Friday, and Charles would most likely be back that evening. So when she returned from her long walk, and had sat in Pauline's room for about twenty minutes, tracing the space where she and Alexander had writhed about those weeks ago, she decided she would try to face Charles with a clear head. They would speak rationally again, and she would not hide from him in her drunken smokescreen. She had to break the cycle, somehow.

She went down into the kitchen and opened the fridge, only to see that Nelly Harrison had made more duck in orange. She stared at it, and thought she heard a car outside on the gravel. She paused there, the fridge door open, frozen, as she waited for the steps on the stairs. But none came.

Suddenly, a deep desire washed over her, and she knew how she could escape the fear. Annihilation through port. But she had not gone to her little stash in the grotto today for precisely that reason: she wanted to face him with a clear and sober head. He could not be that merry figure that was distant and ridiculous to her. She had to face him so she could enjoy the proper purity of her solitary life at Hartlands.

She struggled with the temptation, and she began to pace up and down the room like a hungry tigress. But Polly was not hungry. She listened. The trees creaked as the wind cooed around the edge of the house. The breeze caught up the fallen leaves with the gravel, and they dragged together like the ghostly steps of dead men.

Polly swallowed, hard. The lights flickered a little. Or she might have blinked, she had no way of telling. Still she paced, the cold hands of fear laying their fingers around the back of her neck, always lurking, always taunting her.

Then a figure appeared at her side. She jumped, suppressing a shriek, and looked around to see the empty air. It must have been a strand of her hair, long and loose, cascading down her cheeks and eyes, fiendishly tricking her. She started to shake, the terror was growing, and all she wanted was a gulp or two or three of port.

She turned from the thought and went down into the snug. The photographs there mocked her. Pauline's face was lurid in her wedding dress, her lips too red, her mouth too wide, parting to swallow Polly whole. Alexander was there too, with his wife, smiling coolly, yet he was so hot and passionate and frenetic, she could not understand it. She could almost feel his flesh as she dug into it with her nails like she would destroy him and have him at the same time. Disgusted and thrilled, she went up the steps into her bedroom, Nelly Harrison's old room.

She sat on her bed and looked at her suitcase, which she still had not unpacked. She had to distract herself from her ticking thoughts somehow, and the suitcase was just the thing. She would choose a nice dress to wear for Charles that evening, and try to act like the lady she was, like the lady she could be. She would show him that she was capable of changing, of getting herself together, and the dress would do just that. It would also trick him out of noticing the tired purple bruises that clung under her eyes like unhappy limpets, the blows which belonged to him, and make her the beautiful alabaster model he had first come upon in the café back in March.

She found the red dress, the one she had worn at the Radisson. It was very much creased, as it had been stowed away forgotten at the bottom of her suitcase. But it would do. It would have to do.

175

Before, she had thought that it would look very nice reclining up in the white room, the white and the red mingling there together. She remembered how she had scoured Pauline's white bed a couple of days later for blotches of red, and finally she found it, a small round stain sat nonchalantly, unaware of the potency of its provenance. She had successfully raided Nelly Harrison's red bucket with all its cleaning implements for a sponge, which she wetted and took to the bed, dabbing away at the stain. It disappeared, because water usually makes the blood flow away.

She took off her jeans and the big woolly jumper, which hid her slim frame from the prying eyes of the trees around Hartlands. She brought the red dress, with its cold satin folds, tumbling down around her. It felt looser, somehow. The little capped sleeves that were tight around her upper arms now hung there limply, and the synched waist was baggy. Polly was the party balloon that had deflated, and lost its bright and novel charm, hanging around unwanted for days after the celebration.

So she found a belt and wrapped it around her waist. It succeeded in bringing the dress tighter to her body. But the capped little sleeves still hung there though, like the hands of a dead man, so she went to the kitchen, and cut them off.

She had inadvertently made a sleeveless little prom dress. The skirt still went down her body with a little kick and a flick to her knees. But whilst before the dress had oozed sophistication, and was the perfect foil to Charles' dashing urbanity, now it would make a pleasant dress for a sweet sixteen. That was not the look Polly was hoping to achieve.

Polly delved back into her suitcase, and seized her little jewellery box. Within it, she found the silver chain that Charles had declared ruined her beauty, but she strung it around her long neck anyway. Then, it might have devalued her charm, for the red of the dress had popped the colours out of her cheeks and made her glow. It was harder this time for Polly to glow, so weak and yellow as she was, a little sapling starved of light and trying to grow in the cemetery at Hartlands with its dank mossy grass, the tall trees around it blocking out all of the light. Now she needed something that would make her sparkle.

But there was a sparkle of spirit that flicked still in Polly's blue eyes. As she stood in the weak light of her bedroom, searching for her make-up case, the necklace found it.

And the distraction had undoubtedly steadied her. But it had also taken her back to the Radisson and the dirty Martini and God how she would like one now, although she knew how she would hate every sip.

Her fingers trembled as she undid the zip of her make-up case, the stick of kohl dropping to the floor with a tiny thud. She bent over, and she thought she heard a thud outside as well. The hairs at the back of her neck tingled, and she dropped the rest of the case onto the floor. She thought of the grotto bathed in the darkness, her sanctuary and retreat from the unknown noises outside and the anxious murmurings that fluttered at her heart.

She took her make-up case and the little travel mirror with which she checked her face every morning up and into the kitchen. She drew out a chair on the cold stone floor and it screeched at her. She trembled; the noise seemed louder than it ought to have been as it reverberated around the room.

She sat down heavily, and looked at her face. Although the kitchen lights were dim they could not hide the yellow and purple ravages that the torture of the past few months had engrained upon her pale skin. But Polly had always been clever in her sparse use of disguise, as she had the knack of softening her alarming beauty and razor-sharp cheekbones.

But tonight, she applied the foundation thickly, rudely almost, in a desperate attempt to cover up the purple shadows underneath her eyes. She held the mirror back, surveying her handiwork. She almost looked like the woman at the Radisson.

Her concentration lapsed, fatally. In the gap between putting down the mirror and looking for something that would restore a little colour to her cheeks, she had remembered the impatient fire that dwelt within her belly, the grotto that was outside in the darkness. She had to reach it, she simply had to.

Her hands shook afresh. But her face was only half complete. Shrouded by the foundation, her eyes looked smaller, whilst her lips were brushed pale, a study in nude. The sight unnerved her, and she shivered. The trees sighed outside, and perhaps she should hurry up, because Charles might be home soon. But she had no way of knowing.

With a great effort, she forced her hands to the mascara and the kohl, using one hand to steady the other, the mirror placed beneath her on the table. She could not afford to make one false stroke; she didn't have the luxury of those make-up wipes that could wash away mistakes so very easily. Last time though her make-up had been washed away in her tears and her blood, and there on the bed where she had woken up a little mask of orange mingled with the dark red stains.

She was done. She blushed up her cheeks, ran a light covering of red over her lips, and yes, she was done. But still Charles would not come.

The night and the wind outside stilled, and it became silent, a heavy type of silence that rung in her ears. Then she fancied that she heard a strange sort of whizzing, a whirring noise, but it was only the fridge beside her getting agitated.

The fiction and the fantasy of putting on the red dress had served only to while away some of the time, whilst the nagging thought of the bottles out in the grotto still drummed away in her ears, as steady as any heartbeat.

She picked up the mirror, her only form of entertainment, and gazed at it, trying to lose herself in her reflection. She felt nothing. The face that gazed back was hers: the thoughts in her head were not.

She stood up and climbed the stairs out of the kitchen, picking up a little torch that hung on the rack of coats as she went. She opened the green door onto the drive, and stepped out into the still night. A single light flashed its response to her steps, encouraging her further out into the dark.

Indeed, everything seemed to be calling Polly outside, lulling her into the grotto, willing her to open up another bottle and to glug it down. Then, the colour would fly to her cheeks and match the redness of the gown. She could fabricate the idea that in the folds of its fabric she was somehow the girl she had been nearly six months ago at the Radisson, so sure, so poised, so absolutely convinced that she would have the house and have the man.

She stepped further out onto the gravel. It did not make quite the same sound as she thought it would. Its crunch was much quieter than she had been expecting, but perhaps it was keeping her sins quiet, quiet to the night, and quiet to herself.

In the strapless red dress, she stole round the edge of the house, sombre in its quiet reclining majesty. There was the barest whisper of moon, just tangible through the clouds, and so she needed the torchlight, which jumped back off the sad folds of brambles lying scattered at her ankles, jagged and sharp.

Only when she had gone round the edge of the house, up the ridge and along the little path that was nigh impassable in the high summer, when she would have to grapple with the brambles and the bracken that defiantly littered her way, did she notice that her arms and skin were bare to the night. But it seemed like the grotto was waiting for her, and it closed around her like a dank cloak, embroidered by the sea shells stolen from the seashore long ago.

The torchlight caught the mirrors that hung glittering in the walls as Polly stood surveying the port, which had waited so obediently for her arrival.

Then something in the trees gave a bark. She jumped, her back turned to the entrance of the grotto, as she bent down to pick up a bottle of port.

"Polly!"

It was certainly his voice, the voice for which she had been waiting. It chilled her, and she remained couched, grasping a bottle tightly in her white hands. It was cold, very cold, and it should have sent the shivers running through her, but her whole body was tense, just on the edge of relief, as the voice called out to her again.

She had not heard the car, his car. It was his voice though, sure enough, and she remained still, crouched down in the depths of the grotto that promised to hide her within the folds of its dank deathliness.

He could not reach her here, although why he was calling her name out to the night Polly did not understand. The voice called out again, and then it fell silent, the echo falling away, spent. The old grotto had a funny knack of distorting and hiding sounds; but Polly fervently hoped that he had gone back into the house again.

Polly was thirsty, so very thirsty and desperate that the bottle trembled precariously in her hands. She undid the rich red peel that surrounded the cork, and then she gave a deep sigh. She had not thought to bring the corkscrew with her.

But the lust in Polly's veins had risen, and what with Charles lurking about unseen in the night like some ghoul intent on haunting her, she could not help it. She smashed the neck of the bottle down onto the smooth stone of the grotto floor. He might hear the smash of the broken glass, but then again the grotto may have hidden the sound from him.

She brought the broken neck of the bottle to her lips, stained as they were with a hint of Rimmel red. The whole bottle and the liquid within it juggled about impatiently. Her hands were impatient, her body was desperate, and she had to bring the broken bottle to her lips. She felt its jagged edges rest on her lips, they dug in, firmer, tighter, so they cut into her lip when she tipped the bottle back and let the liquid fall down into her throat, fire quenching fire.

And so it was that in her eagerness she did not notice the sharp edges of the bottle splitting open her lip. The port was the anaesthetic she needed to forget everything. She was meant to be sober tonight, though, to see him. But she had never actually wanted to see him that night, grinning in his careless urbanity, a relic shelved high in the archives labelled 1955.

She gulped down the port as if she could forget him. She tipped the bottle back further, further, and the jagged edges bit rabidly into her lips once more. Only then did she feel the affront of the pain through the abyss of the anaesthetic that was pounding through her blood like hemlock. The pain was sharp, and was it blood trickling down her chin again? She knew the feeling, it was warm, warm and wet, not cold like this molten liquid that was thumping through her throat and into her empty churning stomach.

In her disgust she brought the bottle away from her lips, but she brought it away too quickly. She dropped it, and it smashed beneath her. The port jumped up with flailing arms to embrace her red dress, lashing at her bent knees, which shook with the strain of having been crouched there for so long.

It was inevitable that she was going to have to go back into the house. In order to survive the journey, however, she needed more port. Short of slipping down to the ground and lapping the red liquid off the cold stone floor she picked up another bottle, slung it under her arm, and stood up.

Then there was her lip. She wasn't sure whether it was still bleeding, but she didn't know how to check. Her hands were full with the bottle of port and the torch, but in the end her curiosity won out and she brought the hand that carried the torch to her lips. The torchlight wobbled, and sure enough, her lip was still bleeding. She must look a sight.

But there was an inevitability about it all. She would have to go back down into the house and see Charles, and he would most probably laugh at her, she knew he would.

Still the port had failed to numb both her pain and her fears, and she felt cold with her naked shoulders exposed to the night, and the port sticking like clammy seaweed onto her legs.

She clambered down the ridge. Turning back onto the drive, she shivered as a fresh blast of wind saluted her arrival.

His car was there, that silver Aston Martin, vintage of course, like the port she carried in her arms and had stained all over her. If she had not wanted the port so much she would have smashed it over the car, parked there so elegantly, so effortlessly, so amazingly timeless, so much a part of Charles, as the house was, as her dress was, as everything here was.

But she wanted the port so much. She knew that if she got into the kitchen she could find the corkscrew, and that was all that mattered.

In her frenzied haste she moved to the door, dropping the torch as she fought to undo the temperamental latch. She kept a tight hold on the bottle though, and her light steps crashed back down into the kitchen.

She saw him at the table, his back to her, and she might as well get it all over and done with, and smash his head in with a bottle, and hope that he would die. Then she would leave in his Aston Martin, and flee the country. But she could not drive, she had no money, and the only strength that lurked within her was the urge that drew her to the drawer where the corkscrew was.

Charles had come home and had been unable to find Polly in the kitchen. She wasn't in the white room either, or in the snug, or even in Pauline's room. He was amused. Perhaps she had done a runner. It wasn't inconceivable. The gates to the drive were never locked, and from there it would be easy, down along the main road and onto Petworth to seek solace in the arms of that rather vulgar mother of hers, with her dark hair and dark eyes and wrinkled skin like a dirty old rag.

The door flung open and Polly clattered down the stairs. Charles swung round in his chair, relieved and tense, all at the same time.

But nothing could have prepared him for this vision of Polly, crazily gasping as she ran into the room, port bottle under her arm. It was like some nightmare parody of the girl she had been at the

Radisson, dressed so exquisitely to meet him that she shone like a garnet or a ruby.

Charles was even rattled to see her standing there, blood ebbing from her lip, dripping down her chin and neck to settle on her non-existent cleavage. Her bare legs were splattered, the hem of her dress sagged down, and where she had cut the sleeves off the dress a ragged seam remained. The dress, although held up in part by the belt, had begun to fall down so that he could see her black bra beneath. She looked like a sickly autumnal leaf, and was an unreal shade of pale.

She took a fleeting look at him, and made a run for the drawer, bringing out the corkscrew and shoving it into the top of the bottle. Her fingers shook, and the corkscrew would not respond. She put the bottle down onto the blue marble counter with a ringing clash, and yanked at the bottle again. Having removed the cork, she took the port to her lips, and bliss poured into her veins. She could now at least feel some type of peace.

"Playing at vampires now, are we?" Charles mocked, appalled and amused in equal measure.

Polly continued to gulp down the port, her long neck quivering with the effort. There was something vampiric about it though, Charles was right, the woman in her red dress, pale as death, choking down red liquid into her dead veins. But Polly did not, could not, hear him above the din of her intoxicated numbness.

"Polly, you look a sight!" he exclaimed, although he was watching her now with tired, bored, eyes.

He had succeeded. He had succeeded in destroying womanhood, just as he had succeeded in vanquishing life and replacing it with harrowing addicted death, death in a bottle. But it had done nothing to quench the pain he felt bruising him every day when he woke up. Pauline was gone, and she was not coming back. And Polly had become Pauline just as long as she gulped down the port like a rabid beast, hot for blood, but she would never actually *be* her, and he could not hurt Polly as he wanted to hurt Pauline. He had thought that by destroying Polly he could destroy Pauline. He was wrong. It had done nothing to appease his loss. To that end, Charles was beginning to feel uncomfortable as he watched Polly, who continued to furiously guzzle at the bottle like a hungry puppy.

"I knew there was an animal somewhere in you, Polly," he mused, eventually, when her thirst was spent, and she looked at him with wild unseeing eyes.

"Don't you understand?" she spluttered, marshalling the words out of her dead-eyed ecstasy of nothingness.

"Understand what?" he asked, sipping at his whisky like a demure schoolgirl.

"This, this is my resistance," she drawled, slurring the syllables together like a snake.

She was swaying slightly, and she had to grip onto the marble edge of the work surface to steady herself.

"Resistance? Against what?"

Charles sounded amused, and he sipped again at his whisky.

"You, of course!" she replied, fumbling around in the recesses of her shattered thoughts for her reasons, for her logic. Yes, that was it, she was resisting him, defying him, she would not be his jewel.

"It's you, Polly, it's you, you only have yourself to blame."

His voice hung in the room like the bored hum of a bumblebee in midsummer.

"No," she persisted, exhausted, "I'm not your jewel."

"So you'd break the terms of our conversation at the Radisson? Look at this, all around you," he shot back, coolly and cruelly, "I've given you a home here, a wonderful home, in leafy, beautiful, Sussex. A housekeeper to cater for your every whim. I have given you space and distance while I worked in London to keep you in this splendour. Pity me, won't you, when I come home from my toils to find my beautiful young wife mad as a bitch on heat to drink herself to death? Every weekend I come home to find some fresh folly, when you have all that you ever wanted. You knew it was going to be like this, Polly, you knew it all. I kept nothing from you. But no, I come back to find you asleep in my ex-wife's bed, like you've got some kind of strange bond with her. You cower from my friends and treat them like you're mad, or you prefer to play with your stepson's old dinosaur toys. The strain must be very hard for you Mr Carraway, I don't know how you cope."

His voice was liquid silver as it taunted its way through Polly's trembling frame. She could not mount her defence, as his reasoning suddenly appeared completely insurmountable.

"And I thought I had a jewel, something perfect I could stow away, just for me," he mused, watching as she turned to bend herself over the table, her body crumpling like a sad flag drooping in the breeze, fluttering down to an awful stasis.

But as she rested her forehead on the old oak of the table, something clicked in Polly. Out of the intoxicated fog, the magic and the mystique of his words, there finally came clarity.

"You wanted it like this," she mumbled, still bending over, her belt cutting into her, and she fiddled with it to set herself free. "All along you wanted me to crumble. Keep me precious and safe? You would rather that I was destroyed."

Charles looked at her afresh. He was evidently amused that she was stumbling nearer and nearer to the truth.

"You don't buy my philanthropy any more, do you?"

"Your philanthropy disgusts me. It's a bloody sham."

"Well frankly, my dear, I'm disappointed that you took such a short time to crack. And you tell me it's your resistance, but let me tell you something, it's all out of your control. I thought we were better matched, Polly the ice palace, never to be shattered, Polly the ice maiden, never to be thawed."

With some relief, she finally managed to undo the belt that bit into her like Charles' words. The red dress now resembled a torn bin bag as it sagged down further over her thin body, revealing even more of her bra.

She mumbled something incoherent as she continued to lean on the table, striving to hold up her dress with desperate fingers.

"I thought it would be more fun than this, watching you melt. But your vice, sadly, is an obvious one. Who would have thought it? Alcohol! Do you remember what you said at the Radisson?"

In a fumbling gesture, Polly made to push at the air, as if he could just be pushed away, so solid and complete in his chair, so present, so sleek and groomed like his silver Aston Martin lurking out there on the drive.

"No? Or do you mean yes? I don't understand you, Polly. Well, let me tell you anyway. It makes a pretty story, that conversation at the Radisson. I sketched it all out to you then, the isolation, the stasis, and yet you still took it on, despite only seeing one room! Maybe I should have been the one to walk away. But you told me, didn't you, of your pleasure, of your delight in escaping from the vodka-soaked crowds writhing all around you? Your disdain of your so-called friends and their drinking habits, their lack of class, and their lack of self-respect? And look at you now, worse than they have ever been before, I guess. Perhaps you were right to be a virtual teetotal, Polly. You were afraid of the demon that lurks within you. But you're just like everybody else, really, and even worse than them, you're dirt and poison and a hypocrite."

Flesh and the red dress hit the floor with a smothered smack. Polly had fallen in a heap, the dress falling in folds around her, the upper half of her body exposed to him. But she did not cry, nor lapse into the heady balm of those hysterical nonsensical sobs she had found herself wading through the evening her mother had visited Hartlands.

"I am in control of this," she said.

"Delusional, more like," he exclaimed, running his hand down his chin, as if he was surprised at this specimen of femininity that lay defeated before him.

"I did this to spite you, you arrogant bastard," she said, slowly, with some hint of the level reason that had always punctuated her discourse before she came to Hartlands.

She drew her shoulders up, grasping her dress around her like a towel so that it did not slip back off again and reveal her bra.

"I am destroying myself to spite you, you and your philanthropy. How was I supposed to know that you wanted to destroy me too?"

"Put simply, you're out of control," he replied, bored.

"No, no I am not. I can save myself still," she asserted.

She swivelled around from her position on the floor. She was frightening. Her lip had stopped bleeding, but the blood had congealed into a thick lump, where slug-like it perched on her lips. The blood also clung to her neck, and her hair, still long and straight, hung lankly down the sides of her face.

"Anybody might think I'm out of control, you're right, I agree. But I can control it, you'll see that I can."

"You're an addicted mess, Polly, I've never seen someone want a drink so much in my life," he said, and he was positively laughing at her now, ignoring her words with a brush of his hand, as he smoothed down his chino-clad legs.

"I admit, I have a problem, but problems can be solved. I will prove it to you that I am in control, and you won't have won, you really won't have won. You may think that you have, when you think how you tortured me. No television, no Internet, no phone, no mother, no family, no friends. But I glory in my isolation, Charles, I glory in it. It is only you, and it has only ever been you, who I have despised."

The initial ecstatic effects of the port having rubbed off, Polly managed to keep her voice level. It was sinister and calm.

Now she strove to stand, gripping the folds of the red material tightly to her, as she scoured the floor for her belt with which to tie it all back together.

"Oh for heaven's sake put some clothes on. You look revolting," Charles drawled, bored, his stomach yearning only for some duck in orange.

Polly turned, and went down into the snug.

"You will find that I can control the situation," she repeated.

But he had not heard her. He had gone to the fridge, whilst she was in the snug.

Polly then ran into her room. She would finish this, she would end this, she would rid herself of her addiction and throw it down the ridge. She would not let him win.

Her dress was still slipping from her, but she did not take it off. Instead, she bundled herself into a big woolly jumper. She took a deep breath, fighting her dizzying need for more port. Although it had stopped numbing the pain, she saw what she must do.

She returned to the kitchen. Charles was hovering by the AGA, evidently waiting for the duck to heat up. She saw him, and pitied him. But he was distant to her now though, stood over by the AGA as he waited. He did not look up.

In the days that followed Polly wondered what might have happened had he not followed her out into the cold November night. It did not do to dwell on it though, surely.

She remembered feeling vaguely sorry for him then, as she walked through the kitchen. She pitied him because he thought that he had destroyed her, when she had enjoyed the perverse temporary pleasure of destroying herself. She knew she was going to emerge from this, put the pounds back on, and spend them, too. Charles knew nothing of her plan, and how his well groomed gentility was finally going to be rendered futile. He was always a relic, and relics cannot act. It was sad, really, and Polly felt it during that split second in which she returned to the kitchen, the blood still caked on her throat, the port still stuck to her bare legs.

She dashed up the steps and opened the door. She found the torch she had dropped down onto the gravel. She picked it up and ran. Although he might not have seen her in the kitchen, he must have heard her gambolling up the stairs. But Polly didn't spare a thought for him and what he might be doing.

She ran round the edge of the house, up the ridge, and along to the grotto. Breathless, ignoring the brambles that dragged at her ankles like snotty children pawing at their mothers' skirts, she had arrived. She looked about her, her chest heaving, as she flashed the torch around the folds of the grotto with a frenetic flick of her wrists. In the far corner were the bottles of port she had taken from him, and beneath her, the bottle she had broken. She stood there, considering, for what must have been a full minute.

She was considering how best it should be done, and suddenly, she seized upon it. Stepping out of the grotto, she brought the torchlight to the earth, sweeping it through the dead bracken and under the desperate brambles. She found it, a large jagged stone. She picked it up, shaking. Although she knew she had little strength left in her – she was hardly eating, and she was always being sick – the thought of proving Charles wrong was fuel enough for her exhausted limbs. So she began to hurl the stone at the bottles, and they cracked, bleeding out port onto the smooth stone floor beneath.

However, their haemorrhaging was too slow, too gradual, too restrained. Polly was frustrated so she picked up the other bottles, and hurled them to the ground, cursing him as she did so, ignoring the shards of glass that crashed around her like a symphony, and the splashes of liquid that leapt up to stain her jumper, high enough even to wet her lips. Impassively, the ancient shells watched on, as they too were stained by the port that splashed furiously around the grotto.

Perhaps Charles might hear her. But Polly did not care. Anyway, she was hidden away high up in the grotto, so why should he come? The wind was still, as impassive as the grotto, hanging limply in the air. The sound would not travel.

Her frenzy was spent now. She stood still, running the dull torchlight over what she had done: the dozens of broken bottles, the stone floor an ocean of red, her shoes ruined, surrounded by a ring of jagged glass shards.

Bending down, she picked up one of the shards and observed it. She rolled up the sleeve of her big baggy jumper, and traced the shard lightly up her bare arm. She held it gingerly, letting it gently graze her skin. Her death would be too good for him, she mused, as she held it at the perilous point, at the top of her wrist, where she could see the tired veins, and the vital purple arteries buzzing beneath.

But she might just dig the shard in, just there. She might just end it all, lying down in this bath of port. It would look good in the papers, surely. *The Daily Mail* would have a field day. *Beautiful Graduate Found Dead With Wrists Cut In A Pool of Port*. She could see the headlines now.

But it would not just be a pool of port, it would be a pool of her own blood, too. How would the port and the blood mingle? Would it be like the water that just washed it away, easing it so carefully and gently off from her skin? What would it look like to see the blood and the port merging merrily beneath her as her life drained away?

But Polly knew that she was not going to have to immolate herself in order to vanquish him. She was not Lucretia, ravaged by Tarquin, falling on her sword, the phallic irony. She had destroyed her addiction, and the smell was heady, suffocating, as the rich redness of the port rose up and into the night air.

She turned back to go into the house, pleased with what she had accomplished, although her bare legs smarted with the cold and the licks of alcohol.

The speck of moon invited her back out onto the path, and she held the torch so its light hung low. But she wasn't to know that the strange combination of the ridge and the grotto had hidden from her ears the distinctive crunch of the gravel on the drive below.

Charles was ranging round the side of the house, climbing up the ridge, and there he stood before her, shrouded in the darkness, only his feet illuminated by Polly's torch.

CHAPTER FOURTEEN

It was Sunday morning in Petworth. The weekend had been one of those glorious winter weekends of pure blue skies and piercing cold. The welly-clad locals had been on patrol through the parks and along the footpaths, and the little town was gearing up for an influx of more of the same. Little did they know that they would be waking up to the news that would render their town infamous, that had the potential to make it a tourist magnet for lovers of the salacious and the macabre, that would, for better or for worse, affect its property prices for at least the next decade.

One of the leading local ladies was a woman named Patricia Dawson. Patricia Dawson was revered in the area for her interest in charity and the arts, but everybody in the town was well aware that Patricia Dawson knew everybody and anybody locally, and that a word from her was enough to open doors and close them too. It would be unfair to think of Patricia Dawson as a harpy, for she was cultured and to some degree educated, but she was the leader of an incredibly niche kind of society, which boasted, although not explicitly, of more rituals and customs than the Freemasons.

Now of course Patricia Dawson knew Moira Andrews, because she knew everybody. But she was most particularly acquainted with Moira Andrews because Moira Andrews was her next door neighbour. Patricia Dawson and her husband lived on the same cobbled street, where they had downsized after selling their large pile a couple of miles away, after the boys had flown the nest and gone onto better things, like running the banks and the country.

Patricia Dawson did have a habit of looking down on other people, although Moira Andrews was very difficult to look down upon. It was more that business of her unfortunate daughter and Charles Carraway. Of course it was an awful shame, when everybody remembered Pauline, Patricia Dawson amongst them. Moira Andrews' daughter was undoubtedly an opportunist, after the fortune, but that did not stop Patricia Dawson visiting Moira Andrews to discover the latest news about the girl whom she so heartily disapproved.

It was an unpleasant business, but it was not exactly at the forefront of Patricia Dawson's mind when she stepped down the hall to retrieve *The Mail on Sunday*. She was thinking how frightful it was that her favourite paper was now including so many supplements, but she lost that particular train of thought when she noticed the headline emblazoned across the front page. It was impossible to ignore.

Newlywed Professor Found Dead After Stately Home Plunge

Now, like the rest of the Petworth locals, Patricia Dawson had not seen Charles Carraway for a long time. But, as is well known by now, Charles Carraway had aged well, like good wine, and so she recognised the picture provided by his devastated university department almost instantly.

"Oh my goodness, Dennis!" Patricia called, rushing into the kitchen where her much maligned husband sat in his slippers eating a boiled egg.

The aforementioned Dennis barely looked up, accustomed as he was to his wife flitting about the house as if London Bridge was burning down all over again.

"It's Charles Carraway, he's dead."

Before Dennis had time to interject, because he did not know the name and wondered why his wife was in such a flap, Patricia began reading out the article to him.

"Professor Charles Carraway, fifty-seven, the millionaire academic, was found dead yesterday morning by his wife, Polly Carraway, twenty-one.' That's Moira Andrews' daughter, Dennis, you know, the divorced lady who lives next door. Black hair, the old Volvo? You know the one, Dennis," Patricia paused for breath, before continuing to read the article aloud, "Professor Carraway was found at the foot of a ridge on his sprawling country estate near Petworth, West Sussex. Initial reports suggest that his death is not suspicious and the police are not looking for anyone else at this time in connection with his sudden death."

Patricia looked at Dennis, eyes wide.

"Do you think I should pop round, and see Moira? It must be very hard on her."

Patricia did not wait for Dennis to reply. She was already out of the house, onto the cobbled street, and knocking on her bereaved neighbour's door.

Moira opened it, as breathless as Patricia, and obviously relishing the drama of being the mother-in-law to the poor crumpled dead man.

"Thank you for popping by, Patricia. It's just dreadful. I've been over there and poor Polly was in such shock, coming across his body like that. Why they didn't fence that ridge off, it's like a cliff, I have no idea. And his face, all smashed up like that. But apparently he would go out at night on those rambles, or so the housekeeper told me, nice woman, I think her name is Nelly. The police found all these bottles smashed up in some grotto on the ridge, but they think that's just local youths, and has nothing to do with his death. There's no evidence of foul play whatsoever, but poor Polly is understandably very shaken up by it all. And between you and me, Patricia, I think she might be pregnant."

For once in her long reign, Patricia struggled to get a word in.

"Is there anything I can do?"

"That's very sweet of you, Patricia, but I think we've got it all under control. It was such a shock, though, and I feel bad, I do, that I left her there all alone with him. But fancy, her going out for a walk on that lovely morning yesterday and finding his body there all mangled. Poor poppet, she didn't have a phone with her, and the only way she could call the ambulance was to take Charles' out of his pocket! Poor child, widow at twenty-one, rolling around in that big old house."

"I know you'll have so much to do, Moira, anything we can do to help. And you couldn't let me know when the funeral is going to be? Dennis and I should like to attend. We were Charles and Pauline's most particular friends," Patricia asked, swelling up with the importance of knowing the dead man and his ex-wife.

"I will, Patricia, I will. I don't imagine there's anything you can do to help though, as the family is dealing with most of it. Uncle Anthony is coming down today to sort it out, he's some kind of lawyer apparently, and was in contact almost immediately. There'll be some type of inquest, I imagine, a formality, of course. It just seems like the most dreadful accident. I just hope Polly will leave that big old place, it gives me the creeps, and get a nice sensible job in London, like your boys. Personally, although I don't like to speak ill of the dead, and I know he was your friend, I think it's the best thing that could have happened to her. But I've got to go now, I left poor Polly with that housekeeper woman who was most insistent that she would stay to look after her. I better be getting over to Hartlands now."

And then Moira shut the door, almost in Patricia's face.

It had all happened so quickly really, like Moira had said. There hadn't been that much time to think. She found his frosted body at the foot of the ridge from where he had fallen the night before.

When she had woken up that morning, she had almost forgotten what had happened that evening, but she knew that she felt fresher and freer than she had done for months. So when she walked into the kitchen she ceased to feel the oppression of being trapped down beneath the earth. Indeed, as she surveyed the room with fresh eyes, she even started to like it, and then she went to the cupboard and fetched herself some Weetabix. But by the time she had poured the milk over it, and into the bowl, she had remembered.

She went calmly to the shower though, and when she peeled off her nightdress, she saw how her legs were sticky with a red congealed mess. The port must have stained her all over.

And it was difficult, in the shower, to get the port off her. The shower was cold and the port did not come running off her like the blood. It was stubborn, and it needed soap, soap to eradicate it from her skin and to mask the stench, and to finally shove it away down the plughole.

She scrubbed until her skin was red raw, aching in the cold of the shower. Finally, she was satisfied, and she felt clean at last.

She put on one of her favourite outfits: the deep purple skirt, with the trim white blouse, and the belt she had to bring in tighter to make the whole arrangement stick together. Then she put on the green Barbour jacket, and the grey beanie hat, and struck out into the beautiful pure sunlight of the late November morning.

Polly did not feel anything when she saw him lying there like that. But she knew well enough what she ought to do, and so she sent a shivering call to 999. They were good to her, when they arrived, and carted him off stiff into the ambulance. Meanwhile, she was shaking like a leaf because she wanted some port, but they just thought it was the shock. They arranged for her mother to come, but Nelly Harrison arrived first.

The police could not get much from Polly. She confirmed that he had come home late last night, and that he had gone out for a walk. They lived separate lives, and he was often going about the place alone. She did not know what he did. The police presumed she was in shock, and let her grieve.

Nelly Harrison was an invaluable resource, though. She told them that Charles was always walking about the estate, most especially at night. He was one of those academic types, and apparently it helped him to clear his head whenever he came back from London. The police nodded, sagely.

They had come across the smashed port bottles, and they asked Nelly Harrison about them too. They did not want to disturb the widow about so trivial a matter. The housekeeper said Charles liked to keep them out there in the grotto, as the temperature helped them to breath. He was a port expert after all, as well as an academic. It was probably local youths; they often came up to the grotto and smoked there. It was a favoured spot for them.

The police told Nelly Harrison to keep an eye on Polly until her mother came, and then they left them in the kitchen together.

Polly looked steadily across at Nelly Harrison. She sipped at the strong sweet tea that had been made for her, and continued to survey the housekeeper with consummate astonishment sketched out across her pale countenance.

"Why?" she asked, thinking only of Nelly Harrison and her lies to the police.

"Don't you worry, my girl," Nelly Harrison said, with just the smallest hint of affection in her old Sussex voice, "I shouldn't wonder you drank the way you did."

Polly shook her head, uncomprehending still.

"Let's just say, between us mind, that he was a dirty bastard. The way he treated Pauline nearly made me want to kill him. He used to hit her too, you know, although she always used to bounce back up again. That was her way, but it weren't right. I knew I shouldn't get involved, and I didn't, but it didn't stop me noticing it, going on before my very eyes. And then the same with you, although you weren't as tough as Pauline. But you survived, didn't you? You survived."

Just as Nelly Harrison had finished talking, Moira arrived, and shattered her daughter's communion with the housekeeper. Immediately, Polly ran over to the toilet to be sick, and then fell, exhausted, into her mother's arms.

Although intent on comforting her youngest born, Moira would not stay at Hartlands that night. The place frightened her, cowed her, and so Nelly Harrison stayed with Polly instead. She cooked the young widow some sausages, which she wolfed down hungrily, and watched her as she trembled for the port.

The doctor had given Nelly Harrison some sedatives, and she laced Polly's tea with one. Polly soon fell asleep, and Nelly Harrison watched over her, loyal as all the Nelly Harrisons that had been before her, but this Nelly Harrison would render herself unto the male members of the Carraway clan no longer. It had finished, and it would end.

The days passed, and Uncle Anthony came down, and poked his nose about. He was a top barrister, and very influential, apparently. An inquest was called, and Charles' death was deemed to have been a tragic accident. The family, or what remained of the family, Uncle Anthony and his brother and his children and their wives, were all immensely relieved. The body was released for burial, and the funeral service would take place the following Friday.

But Polly had been lucky, because although Charles Carraway was not a good man, he still had good intentions. She felt like Jane Eyre, cashing in with fairy-tale luck, but without the awful burden of having to look after a disfigured cripple for the rest of her life.

Because, as soon became apparent, Charles had left everything to her. Mrs Polly Carraway was bequeathed the house, and all the assets, amounting to a fortune of well over ten million pounds. There was not a whisper of a mention of Alexander Carraway in the will. Nelly Harrison received a generous stipend for the rest of her life, and Uncle Anthony had been seen to for his efforts as executor. Charles had evidently meant what he said about his philanthropy back at the Radisson, and so Polly became a wealthy widow, as well as a young one.

Of course she struck a striking figure at the funeral, which took place in the village church with its infamous tower. She was wearing black, and Polly always made a challenging statement in black.

Nelly Harrison had driven her over to Chichester, where she had bought a long black coat, and broad black hat. She had wanted a veil, but even she felt that it was too gothic and macabre.

So Polly sat at the front of the church, shaking still. She had not drunk for the whole week. The stress had been great. Her mother, prying around the house, when are you going to sell, darling, when are you going to sell? Her mother did not know the truth, though. Polly guessed she would not like it.

The villagers came in droves to peer at the widowed Mrs Charles Carraway, although many of them had not realised that Charles had remarried after Pauline. They unashamedly gawped at the poised young widow, who struck them as so very thin and fragile. Many thought that she was a heroin addict, and what with the last Mrs Carraway being a pothead, it figured.

Polly was tall in her patent heels, and looked to Nelly Harrison for support. Nelly Harrison cut a strange figure without her loud floral apron, as she had bundled herself into a crumpled trouser suit from a local charity shop.

Although the funeral had clashed with Patricia Dawson's weekly French class, she had decided to come anyway. The future conditional could wait. But in the event she was late, because she and Dennis had bumped into the Norburys on the way over, and they were such darlings, such good friends, were they not going to the funeral too? But the Norburys were giving it a miss – they had only ever really known Pauline – and so Patricia, her husband trailing in her wake, strolled into the church to see the tall rise of Polly's hat towering over the rest of the congregation.

The Carraway family walked out first. Patricia thought it was odd how Polly seemed to see nobody. She was icy and ethereal and completely untouchable, and she was most certainly not grieving.

Moira had seen her, however.

"Patricia, you came," she said crispy, nodding at Dennis, "I'm afraid Polly's taken it all very badly, poor girl. But isn't Charles Carraway's son such a nice young man?"

Moira turned, her voice too loud and too vulgar both for the church with its celebrated tower, and the solemn occasion in which she was participating.

Patricia followed the direction of her glance and saw a devastatingly tanned young man talking quietly with Polly and a lady with frizzy hair, who was dressed in a badly fitting black trouser suit. It seemed insulting to see him flashing his white teeth when his father lay dead in the coffin at the front of the church, reminding everybody of how he was so young and vital and alive.

"We're going off to the burial now, Patricia. Did you know that Hartlands has its own cemetery?" Moira asked, although she did not pause to let her omniscient neighbour respond, "I certainly didn't. But it's family only, I'm afraid, but thank you both for coming. I'm sure Polly appreciates it."

Patricia and Dennis stood back, sidelined, watching as they carried the coffin back up the cold abyss of the nave, and the church drained of its congregation.

Patricia positively bristled. As first lady of the town, it was her right to attend the burial, but then she realised that she had a lunch date with some other grand dames of the area to whom she could provide an account of the whole business, how the widow was high on heroin, how her mother had neither class nor dignity, and how Charles Carraway should never have let Pauline go.

After the burial, Polly stood by the window in the white room, where she had decided to hold a little wake. Nelly Harrison had been invaluable. She had made tea and coffee and little triangle sandwiches, having also sourced some smoked salmon and caviar for Uncle Anthony and his family.

Motionless, Polly continued to stand by the window, as she surveyed the valley, her valley, now that she was mistress of Hartlands at last. Distantly, she heard the burr of conversation, her mother and her sister speculating how much it was all worth, whilst Uncle Anthony spoke in hushed tones to his aristocratic relatives. Polly was stuck in between, and maintained her striking pose, staring and static at the window.

She thought of the port, and buckled, slightly. She had to get out of the room. She mumbled something, off to the loo again, she must be pregnant, and felt herself being drawn to Pauline's room upstairs. Yes, she would claim it as her own room, and she would fill it with new furniture and have it decorated. It wasn't like she was strapped for cash or anything.

As she pondered on how she could improve the room, Polly sat down on the bed. But she was not alone, as Alexander had followed her up the stairs and along to where she sat dreaming.

"So, when are you selling? Your mother seems very keen for you to go."

"I won't be selling," Polly replied, abstractedly, as she laid a proprietorial hand on the coverlet.

"What?"

"I won't sell," Polly repeated, setting her jaw firmly. "I won't leave Hartlands."

"But I'd hoped you'd think of me, and sell up the place, so we could split the proceeds. It's hardly fair of the old devil, disinheriting me like that. I thought you were more decent than him."

Alexander was clearly growing exasperated, grasping at straws. As soon as he heard of his father's sudden death he was on the first plane out of Argentina. He needed money, Rosita needed more polo ponies, the new baby had been born, and he was living far beyond his means. He needed the money, desperately, and although before it had suited his cause to doubt that Charles Carraway was his father, he was now convinced, more than ever, that the dead man was his true parent.

"I'm not going to sell," Polly repeated, with more firmness, as she looked into Alexander's dark eyes.

Alexander took this as a sign, and he bent down to hold her cold cheeks, bringing his lips to hers. For a split second, she nearly gave into the warmth of his touch, but it was only for a second, as she pushed him away, furious.

"You were easy enough when I was last here," he said, thwarted, pacing the carpet like his father had done so many times before. "You're a cold bitch, Polly."

"I know, isn't it wonderful?" Polly breathed, some colour firing up in her cheeks.

Something sparkled in her blue eyes, and he moved to the door, as if he sensed that his whole endeavour had been somehow futile.

"I bet you want me," he taunted, uselessly.

"No, I don't," she replied, steady and certain. "You see, Alexander, it's always been about Hartlands. I'm sorry to say that I never, for one moment, loved or respected your father. In fact, I loathed him. I despised him. But the house, the house is the only thing I've ever felt some kind of passion for. It nearly crushed me, though, he nearly crushed me, but you know what," she continued, smiling, "I've won, haven't I? I've finally won."

Alexander had gone. She did not know for how long she had been talking to herself, crowing over her victory.

Let Alexander contest, but the will was the will and she would keep Hartlands, come what may. From the moment of Charles' death it had come back to life as if she had freed it from a spell, and she marvelled at it all around her. When the death duties were paid, she would set about restoring it. Maybe she would invite Pauline to stay, but Pauline might guess. But she hadn't done anything wrong, really. He had fallen, and she hadn't gone for help, but anybody would have done the same, for Charles had practically signed his death certificate that night at the Radisson.

"Just so you know," he said, as she was slipping her black cardigan on, so that she was ready to plunge back out into the mild June night, "I've already taken the liberty of changing my will."

She looked at him, questioningly.

"I'm leaving everything to Mrs Polly Carraway. And I mean everything. The house, the assets, everything."

He kissed her cheek, although she knew he would never touch her again, and she ran all the way back to her house up on the viaduct, aflame with a wild passion.

"Ah, I see you have found the grotto. You two are kindred spirits, I suppose," he drawled, always drawling and drowning in his own poisonous scorn.

He had blocked her way on the path. He had pushed her so that she stood dangerously close to the edge of the ridge, with her back to it.

Polly shivered, feeling the chill of the expectant oblivion behind her, the cold draw of the shell lined grotto down along the path, and the colder soul of Charles Carraway stood there in front of her.

She drew her feet back so they clung to the edge of the drop. Charles looked down at them, curious, but then she flashed her torch round, back to the grotto, illuminating it so that he could see what she had done.

"I am in control," she said, simply, as she trembled all over.

The chill of the November night crept all over her body. She was shaking, almost uncontrollably.

She brought the torchlight over the messy myriad of broken bottles. The stone floor of the grotto was thick with port, as it struggled to drain away, to escape the grotto and run back into the earth.

Charles said nothing, and smirked, slightly.

"I want a divorce," Polly explained, as she stood out there in the night, the steep drop looming like a phantom behind her.

"I won't agree to it."

"You'll want to," Polly replied, as she ran her eyes over the dark lines of Hartlands. "Once you know what I've done."

"You're an alcoholic who, in a fit of remorse, has destroyed my priceless port collection. It's hardly grounds for divorce, is it? And besides, when you've got all of this around you, what you really love, why ever would you want to leave it? Come on, Polly, enough of this. Let's go inside."

"I'll take all of this, I will," she said, and the strength of his grip on her arm intensified.

Then, he laughed. He stood there, and laughed. It mocked her, her and her little comment as it floated up and away into the air between them, onto the dark walls of Hartlands, flitting off the ridge to find fresh flight amongst the firs.

"My dear," he began.

Perhaps he was not going to give a damn. Perhaps he was going to throw her down the stairs, or shoot her, and bury her body at sea in an old leaky yacht.

"I can't let that happen."

She knew that it was now, or never. She dashed forward in a quick movement, pulling his arm away from hers. Frail and lean, she dodged him, but he had lunged fatally forward as he tried to stop her. She turned around, and watched him as he fell, screaming, to his death.

"You know what," she said. "You've always been the problem with this place."

She heard a howl, as he seemed to curse the life that he was leaving, but she kept on running. She would not turn back now.

She ran down the ridge, tripping between the debris of summer. As she encountered the gravel of the drive, which shrouded the sound of his screams, she became relieved.

She ran into the house, and into the kitchen, where she threw off her clothes, the big old jumper and the red Radisson dress. She shoved them into the fire in the snug, adding more firelighters as she did so, stabbing at them with a poker so they burnt up quicker.

Then, exhausted, she dived into her bed to find perfect solace in the fresh sheets. She pulled the duvet tight and right up above her head, and there she slept for the first time in months, a deep proper sleep.